2012 Armageddon:
Unholy Alliance

Preisler Harrington

Dedicated to my family

Copyright © 2011

Cover Design by Judy Ballard

Introduction

'2012 Armageddon: Unholy Alliance,' A.K.A. *'The Nuclear Sword of Damocles'* (alternate title) has been reedited. I hope the changes have made this story more enjoyable.

The prophecies and myths surrounding doomsdays cause many of us to reflect upon our lives and our own mortality. I want to make it clear there are good and honorable people in every culture that strive to live in peace with others, but there are also those who are consumed with hatred, harboring warped visions of segregated societies and delusions of themselves as masters of the universe or even the hand of God. History has recorded a multitude of these scenarios and they never end well. Pain, suffering, and slaughter- all for some pile of dirt, a bigger share of the resources or ethnic cleansing in the name of our Creator. This is one such scenario.

October 2009

When Jordan opened her e-mail she saw the letter she had been dreading all week. It was a response to her three hundred-seventy-fifth job application this year alone, and yes, it was another rejection letter.

This rejection was from the Komuta Corporation, an institution that conducts research that combines cultural data with defense policy. With a B.A. in Anthropology and a M.A. in U.S. National Security under her belt, Jordan considered herself a perfect fit for the job.

Sitting at her computer desk contemplating what her next move would be, Jordan found herself preoccupied with the rambling thoughts of why she had been consistently rejected. *Could it be my age?* Jordan was already in her late forties. *Could it be that I am female?* Even in the 21st century, this was still an exceedingly male dominated field. *Could it be my lack of experience?* Jordan hadn't found a job since she earned her B.A. three years ago.

Jordan was proud of her ability to analyze facts and assess a situation without getting emotional. Her calculating demeanor sometimes put people off, but not Leonard, her devoted and understanding husband of thirty-one years. Leonard's position as an active duty U.S. Coast Guardsman meant they transferred to a new duty station about every three years. They had just arrived at yet another new station, this time in The Hamptons on Long Island, New York. This constant moving had made it quite difficult for Jordan to establish a solid career. As the thoughts seemed to tackle each other to be heard, Jordan's cell interrupted her trance with the chorus of "Anxiety." That was her mother Lillian's special ringtone. Chosen so Jordan could ignore it without even looking at the caller ID.

"Hello?" Jordan said distractedly.

"Hey sweetie! It's your mom- why did you take so long to answer the phone?" Lillian nasally squawked.

"Uh, I don't know… Um, I was outside…" Jordan sighed, now regretting answering the phone.

"Did you hear yet? Did they schedule an interview?"

"Uh, nope. They're not interested."

"It just really seems like a waste of all that money you spent on school, I mean, you're just a housewife and mother like me, but I didn't pay one hundred thousand dollars to do this!" Lillian harped on. "Maybe this is for the best. Why you don't just get a normal, everyday job- be a teacher like your sister! Listen, you're married, why would you want all the stress that comes from a man's job? You should go to work, do what you're told and then go home to your husband." Lillian obviously hoped this was the time Jordan would finally just give up her "crazy dream."

That was not going to happen.

Jordan mumbled, "Yeah, why would I want to be educated enough to understand human behavior, intelligently analyze the complexities of civilization and possibly contribute to humanity…"

"What? Did you say something, dear?" Lillian chirped.

"No, Mom, not a thing, as usual." As if Jordan would be heard anyway. Best to change the subject.

"Mom," Jordan said, "how about we come over this weekend and have dinner with you and Dad. The boys would be happy to spend another evening with Roland."

Jordan's brother-in-law, Roland, was married to her sister, Carrie. Roland was a well-known studio musician, and since most of Jordan's boys were musicians too, it made for some wonderful evenings.

Roland and Carrie had recently moved in with Lillian. Roland had had very little work lately and Carrie had been laid off after eighteen years of teaching at a nearby community college. Their two daughters, Megan and Janice, had both been in college, but the money shortage had forced them to come home indefinitely. Lillian and her husband Ed already had a full house with her mother, Anne.

The economy had hit everyone hard in the past six years and more than one family member had lost their home. Most of Jordan's sons were back home for the same reason. Her oldest son Thomas was twenty-eight, tall, with beautiful dark hair and had always been someone who worked with his hands. Sometimes he felt a bit out of place around so many people who were well educated, but not in front of Jordan. Jordan had always told him he was smart and talented, and that working with his hands was how his intelligence expressed itself. He had just been laid off from the cable company and recently gotten divorced after eight years of marriage to his ex-wife, Diane. They had one child together- Seth, a beautiful three-year-old. Thomas had custody of Seth.

Marshal was Jordan's second son. When Marshal was young, he had been kind of a "Dennis the Menace"- with a healthy dose of hyperactivity and escape artist added in. He was blonde, green-eyed, handsome, strong, and extremely talented in sports, although he never followed through with the opportunities he was offered. Marshal had met and married his wife Chloe while working at a burger place when they lived near San Francisco. He had moved back home after getting laid off from a grocery store a few months back with Chloe and their dog, a boxer named Thor. Thor didn't exactly see eye to eye with

Jordan's boxer, Kaila. Chloe was pregnant with their first child- a boy.

Jordan's third son, Wesley, had been attending Connecticut College until this past June. He was a gentle giant at six feet, three inches tall, blonde, blue-eyed and very quiet. He harbored a secret talent for rapping, and was an expert at *Call of Duty*. During high school he had been very active in sports, but except for an occasional game with Leonard and the other boys, he stayed glued to his computer or TV. He no longer had enough money to go back to school. Prices had been rising for years for consumer goods, resources and education. His school had more than doubled its tuition and fees in the past three years. Wesley was supposed to have started his senior year, but school loans had all but been suspended and most of the students left were those whose parents could afford to pay cash. He moved in during the summer like usual, but this year he was not going back to the dorms.

Jordan's youngest son, Jay, was a sophomore in college, studying to be a nurse. Although all of Jordan's sons were exceptionally bright, Jay was the one who wanted to use that to his advantage. The supply of nurses in the U.S. had dwindled over the past decade, driving demand up. Previously the U.S. had imported nurses from the Middle East, Asia and South Africa, but restrictions on work visas had tightened due to national security concerns. Consequently, nursing was one of the only fields for which scholarships were still available. Jay was still in school and living in the dorms at nearby Stony Brook University, but he still enjoyed coming home every weekend.

Candace, Jordan's firstborn and only daughter had attended college for two years before she dropped out to get married. She had been married nearly six years before she had Jordan's first grandchild, Ashley. Ashley was just eighteen months old and an absolute cutie. Candace's husband, Richard, was a skilled craftsman and was luckily still employed. The company he worked for, Leland Industries, built fighter jets for the military. With a war on, Richard's job was as secure as it could be. Jordan's unemployment meant spending extra time with Ashley, but the family really needed her to be earning income. Right now Jordan's house had seven adults, one child and two pets living under one roof with currently only one income.

Jordan was organizing for the weekend trip to Lillian's house, which was just two and a half hours away. Lillian's husband Ed was a retired State Police Detective who still volunteered on cold cases during his spare time. Having the extra people in the house made it very challenging for Lillian and Ed to provide for everyone's needs, but they thanked God their home had been in the family for many generations and wasn't mortgaged. Jordan had just finished the shopping list for the weekend at Lillian's when Leonard came in from work.

"Hey, sweetie, how was your day?" Jordan asked.

"All right, but we do have to talk later, in private. How was your day?"

"Well, I certainly need to talk too- I'm glad you're home," Jordan said as they embraced and kissed like a couple of teenagers, prompting Seth to tease: "Get a room!"

Dinner and clean up was as monumental as always, but everyone finally settled down to watch some TV. It was Tuesday so their favorite show, *NCIS* was on. *NCIS* was also Anne's favorite show. Jordan called her grandma every Tuesday night right before the start of the show, so they could feel like they were watching together. After the show, Jordan called Anne and they talked about the episode for twenty minutes until Anne headed for bed.

"Good night," Anne said to Jordan.

"Night, GG," Jordan replied.

Anne was one of Jordan's favorite people on the planet; Jordan wished she could be with her every day. Anne had lost all of her remaining friends and siblings in the last four years. Sharing the show gave her something fun to look forward to.

Jordan and Leonard went upstairs to shower and get ready for bed. The house was never quite still, even at night. The guys stayed up late dueling it out on their respective computers playing *Call of Duty* with hundreds of other unemployed online gamers. Jordan and Leonard always played a CD of ocean waves during the night to keep the sounds of war and barking commands at bay. After they made love, they lay back in the bed and shared the details of their day. Leonard hadn't wanted to ruin the evening, but now it was time to tell Jordan the bad news.

"Well, I've got some bad news. I heard that since insurance companies, even the military's insurance carrier, had to start covering older children up to age twenty-six who were still in school, we will have to start paying a premium or cost share." Leonard's tone was worried.

Jordan began to realize that what she wanted to talk to Leonard about would need no further discussion. "Babe, I was going to talk to you about my job search. I'm being rejected by everyone- it's seriously weighing on my self-esteem," Jordan joked feebly, trying to lighten the mood. "I'm contemplating giving up, just quitting. It's like I'm beating my head against a wall every day. I'm not marketable. I thought I had something of value to give to the world, but I guess I'm mistaken. The time and money I spend on job hunting could be spent on you and the kids. It seems everything I do costs us something! An education and a great job was wishful thinking. There's nothing to show for it all."

Leonard interrupted, 'global coooooling.'

"You're silly Leonard," Jordan said. Leonard takes phrases like 'global warming,'a catch all for everything that is wrong in the world and reverses it. He thinks it is funny and he does it to get Jordan out of a mood that is spiraling downward.

"I want you, short one. You are everything to me. Someday college and all this searching will pay off for our family somehow, I just know it. I also *want* you, if you know what I mean," Leonard said flirtatiously as Jordan settled into his embrace.

That weekend came, and the whole entourage drove over to Madison to Lillian's house. Megan and Janice were home from Boston and had settled into a room that had been finished off in the basement. Megan and Janice were disappointed to leave Boston. Both girls had been attending Boston College and had made a life for themselves there. They had been sharing an apartment with two other students and splitting everything four ways. They had friends, school, and were involved with local musical theater. The girls didn't quite understand the gravity of the situation and the sacrifice their parents had already made this past year to fight to keep them in school. Roland and Carrie had started selling a few items from their home and had started skimping on their mortgage payments to help pay their tuition and fees. Roland had sold a vintage guitar that Ray Charles had given him when he worked on a studio session with him. It was something he cherished. He was honestly just happy there was someone who could afford to buy it.

When Leonard and Jordan arrived, the girls had started in on Carrie. They said that Carrie had probably made them come home in some stupid attempt to make herself feel like she was still in control of their lives and could "hold the keys to their future in her hands unless they did as she pleased." Carrie did come off as a bitch quite often, but it was well intentioned. She honestly just wanted the best for the girls, so she was hard on them and demanded a lot. She figured if she was demanding then the world wouldn't run them over, that they would have the advantage over the world through education and attitude. Roland saw her toughness as an opportunity to be the "fun" parent, so he wasn't that supportive of Carrie's stance. This could make Carrie feel quite alone, but she felt her girls' success was more important than her happiness. Carrie was critical of most people and wasn't shy about speaking the first negative thoughts that came to her mind about anybody, but at least with her girls it was truly well intentioned.

"You are so pathetic, Mother. I guess you just couldn't stand it that we were doing all right on our own," said Megan.

"I was finally happy. I was doing great. I can't believe you are so desperate for control, you would actually take us out of school!" said Janice.

"Hey, hey, hey!" Leonard interrupted. "This is a family weekend, not a reality TV show! Lighten up! It's beautiful outside, we are all together, we have a bunch of food and it's not all healthy!"

The boys came in calling out to Roland and they all ran to the garage to play music. Lillian began to complain about the noise of metal guitars, but Jordan interrupted her.

"Mom, that sound is a miracle to me. They are here with us, they are healthy, they are being creative, they feel comfortable enough to share their talent with us, and besides, if it were silent it would mean the boys were gone. I want to be the one who knows what she has before it's all gone. Noise is family, silence is solitude."

Lillian just stared at Jordan, knowing she was right, and attempted to use another excuse. "Jordan, GG is in her nineties. I am sure she doesn't want to hear that kind of 'music'."

Anne yelled out, "It sounds alive and right now that's good thing! Let it play!"

Lillian went about her business with a tiny huff.

Carrie came in and said, "Jordan, any luck on the job hunt?"

Jordan replied, "No, and I am seriously thinking it's not worth the effort. I thought I was doing this to help my family. It's been three years since I graduated with my B.A. and… nothing. Absolutely nothing. All I've managed to do is to create another looming debt. That's really why I started graduate school- to keep from paying the undergrad loans. I mean it, how can education in this economy be worth it when all you can do is create more debt? I thought it would change our lives from living 'paycheck to paycheck' to living with some breathing room. Honestly, Carrie, I don't think I'm employable. No one wants me, even with the graduate degree. I was thinking about suspending my efforts, but I can't. There is so much uncertainty, I just can't give up."

"I know what you mean," Carrie interjected. "I never thought we would be in this situation. I mean, I always knew *you* would be, but us? Roland and I are both professionals and have always taken our education, careers, and future seriously. You're the one that got pregnant and married at eighteen, so it wasn't going to turn out any other way. Starting college in your forties is pitiful, so your professors felt they had to pass you."

Jordan thought to herself, *Well, excuse me, Miss "I did everything right."*

"I mean why would anyone hire you as a new graduate at your age? They are automatically going to assume you were a total screw up or you would have gone to college when you were supposed to go. And why should they invest in a career that will only last maybe five to ten years? You should take a job at a store or something while you wait, because you're probably never going to get a professional position. You're too much of an optimist."

"Thanks, Carrie," Jordan said sarcastically. "I needed a slap of reality, should clear up my confusion in no time."

"Glad to help, sweetie. If you need to talk more, just come see me," Carrie said, leaving the room a little bit darker than when she came in.

Jordan sat there for several minutes trying to persuade herself not to say what she really wanted to say to Carrie, which was: "No wonder your kids call you a bitch." But she had to remember Carrie was a non-apologetic, tough realist, much like her. Jordan calmed herself down and went onto the porch where everyone was having coffee and watching the kids play in the leaf piles. The boys' music was audible in the background. Leonard and Ed were having a serious discussion about Leonard's last deployment on the USCGC Sherman, and the large amount of drugs they had seized. Ed wasn't particularly social, but get him talking about law enforcement operations and he would talk all night. Jordan went over to Candace and asked how they were doing.

"I'm OK, Mom. Richard still has his job- that seems to be the most important issue right now. However, with him working at night I never get to see him! I've been picking up some massages this week, but I can only schedule them when I have someone to watch Ashley. Of course, it has to be family, because I can't afford to pay anyone to watch her, and besides, I don't want strangers to care for her. Therapeutic massage is something you only pay for when you've got money or your insurance pays for it, so business is slow right now," Candace said as they watched the kids. "Mom, Richard and I saw a documentary last week on the Mayan civilization. The program went into all this hype about the world ending because the Mayan calendar just stops on December 21, 2012. Do you think the hype is true?"

"Sweetie, if the world does have an expiration date, do you really think there is something any one of us could do about it?" Jordan asked her.

"No, I guess there isn't, it was just really scary they way portrayed a cataclysmic end, all with vivid graphic scenes," she answered.

"Then why waste one precious minute worrying about it?"

Just then, Ashley ran from the leaf pile, up the stairs and into Jordan's arms. They sat down in the rocking chair.

"Ashley, tell Mema what you did today," said Jordan.

Ashley proceeded to tell her all about it in authentic eighteen-month-old gibberish. Jordan thought it was the most beautiful story ever.

All the kids were put to bed when Roland and the boys came onto the porch with their acoustic guitars. Lillian sat down at the piano near the open window to the porch and everyone started singing oldies. When they surpassed the 70's, Lillian stopped playing. They ended the evening with a campfire version of "Cocaine," which Lillian didn't approve of, but which Anne obviously enjoyed. They all went to bed and the wonderful weekend ended up being too short as always. It felt good to be this close to family again. Leonard's career in the military had kept them on the move and away from family most of their lives.

On Monday morning, Leonard was back at work, Jordan was home with everyone else, and as always, it was hectic. With a full house of different personalities, ages and species, even the simplest routine days of laundry, meals and clean up were more than hectic; they were crazy. Jordan stood in the kitchen after lunch with Marshal and Wesley arguing over whose turn it was to do dishes. She stared at a magnet on her refrigerator that said, "Raising children is like being pecked to death by a chicken." For some reason she thought it would be a little more peaceful at her age, especially considering the boys were now adults.

"Boys," Jordan sighed, exasperated. "Do I really need to take out Mr. Schedule? Honestly!" Wesley gave in (like always) and did the dishes. Jordan was trying desperately to get to her computer to do some more job hunting. Finally, by 3:30 p.m. Jordan was able to get a turn at the computer. She went to her room and locked the door. She had barely gotten the first job site up on the screen when an impatient knock sounded on the bedroom door.

"Mom? Mom? I need you to see this!" Marshal stated as if it were extremely important. "Marshal, I am busy right now, please just give me a half hour and I will come look at it."

"Mom, it is really important- look!" Marshal said as he tried to push a magazine under the door. Jordan stuffed a towel under the door. Two minutes later, Marshal was knocking on her window that was next to her desk. Marshal had climbed out the window in the adjoining bedroom and over the roof. The magazine was open to a picture of a new bike frame. Jordan just held her head as if it were about to fall off her shoulders, gathered her senses and started to giggle quietly. Marshal made her laugh quite often and many times it was his lack of common sense that did it for her. Here he was, living at home with his wife, no job and looking at new, very expensive bike frames! Not even the ones that you would buy for transportation, but for a BMX bike, the kind you use in extreme sports.

"It's beautiful Marshal, but not very practical right now," Jordan finally said.

"I know," said Marshal, "but soon..."

He started to go on and on about how he was going to find a great job real soon and since he was so smart, he would be promoted quickly and... yadda, yadda, yadda. Jordan had heard it so many times. Marshal was a bit of a dreamer, but didn't want to put in the effort to make those dreams come true. Jordan figured eventually his actions would catch up with his aspirations. Marshal finally went away still talking about himself and Jordan was able to get back to her job search. She visited more than ten job sites daily looking for new postings and a few dozen more maybe twice a week. After a few hours of searching, she checked her e-mail before she gave up the computer to the next "desperately seeking employment" family member.

She was going through and deleting all the ads that just seemed to keep coming although she marked them as junk when she saw an official e-mail from the Department of Homeland Security. Jordan had applied to DHS eighteen months ago, and had had two follow-up interviews. Then Jordan had received a rejection notice from them about four months earlier and decided never to apply again. She felt it had been a lot of effort for nothing. She opened the e-mail and it was from yet another "Special Agent in Charge"- an Agent Barrett, someone that she had never met. The letter stated that if she was still interested in a position at the agency to contact him ASAP.

Jordan contacted Agent Barrett and set up an interview with him in his office in New York City. Jordan was nervous, but once again, Leonard put her at ease. Right before she went into Agent Barrett's office, Leonard texted her and reminded her to mention to the Agent that she had just adopted a kitten. Jordan burst out laughing. The previous year Jordan had tried to get a seasonal Christmas job at her local Sears. She had applied three Christmases in a row, but this was the first time she was called in for an interview. She went to the interview and it turned out to be a group interview. There were twenty to thirty people in the room. Several administrative people sat at a desk in the front of the room asking questions that would be answered by all, but one at a time. One of the managers asked this question, "What is your greatest most recent accomplishment?"

Jordan thought to herself, this is a six-week job, you should be able to get this job if you have a pulse. It was her turn to answer and Jordan stood up and stated her best accomplishment was her Master's degree she had earned about five months earlier. Jordan didn't get a job.

The girl in front of her, about twenty-five years old, stood up and said she felt her greatest accomplishment was the fact she had finally begun to learn responsibility in her life because she adopted a kitten. She got a job. At the time it felt like a kick in the head, but Leonard used it as comic relief, which was working very well.

"Hi, I'm Special Agent Barrett. Wow, you're short," Agent Barrett said loudly.

"What?"

"Sorry, I tend to be blunt. You'll need to get used to it if you're going to work for me. The agency has had your resumé for a long time and it's been passed around like a dirty picture. Damn, sorry, again, for that analogy. Anyway, I finally got it last week and I could really use your help. Every aspect of this job can be handled better with some cultural insight, which I don't have. I am an older WASP born and raised in American suburbia. I have a very limited worldview. Your background in Anthropology can add a dimension to my work that I have been told will greatly improve my understanding and interactions with various people."

"I'd be glad to help in anyway I can. Are you offering me the job?" Jordan said hopefully.

"Do you consider yourself to be a patriot?"

"Yes, sir, I do," Jordan said.

"Can you work long hours and possibly travel?"

"Yes, sir." Jordan answered.

"It's yours if you want it."

"Yes, I accept, thank you!" Jordan said with astonishment.

"Jordan, you will be working with a task force of agents focussing on terrorism, child sexual trafficking, slavery and illegal immigration. There's a shit load of paper work that will still need to be done over the next few weeks before you start, but after that you should be good to go, OK?"

"Yes, sir."

"Don't call me sir, Jordan, OK?"

"Yes, sir!"

Jordan decided to share with him the joke about the kitten. Agent Barrett actually broke down laughing which set them on a course for a good working relationship and friendship. Jordan went home eager to share all the details with Leonard.

Leonard greeted her at the door with a bouquet of wildflowers he had picked from the side of the road and a great big hug.

"I knew you could do it. I have always believed in you," Leonard whispered, his voice brimming with pride and love.

"I love you, Leonard. I don't know what I would do without your support and love," Jordan replied. She felt the release of so much hope and work over such a long period of time.

"I am finally employed. I have a title. I am a Criminal Investigator for The Department of Homeland Security."

December 2009

The first day of work finally came and as Jordan made her way out of the train station into the heart of New York City she didn't know what to expect. She wanted to make a good first impression, so she arrived at 7:30 a.m. One of the first things she learned was that no one else got in until 9 or 9:30, at which point they all promptly walked to their nearest Starbucks for coffee. Jordan had always had this vision of "Special Agents," especially at Homeland Security, working 'round the clock, in a state of high alertness and urgency. She had imagined that when she began working there, she would be ushered into a situation room, where a task force was working diligently on several matters at once, making real time decisions to act and deploying agents into the field. This obviously wasn't the case.

The first task that Agent Barrett had Jordan do was to read and memorize the COOP plan. COOP stood for "Continuity of Operations." In other words, how to carry on and conduct daily government business after a disaster, whether it be a natural disaster like an earthquake, flood, or tornado, or an unnatural disaster like a terror attack.

Jordan sat down at her desk and began to read the one thousand page document, taking notes as she went. It was an amazing document and it made references to COG, the emergency plan for the "Continuity of Government." Unlike COOP, COG covered the leadership of the United States- the President, Vice President, Joint Chiefs, Congress and so forth. COG was the face of the government, whereas COOP covered the millions of workers who punch in every day at the alphabet soup of government agencies. The only thing Jordan had ever heard about COG before was regarding 9/11. President Bush had been whisked away on Air Force One after the attacks. The President had been criticized for not being around initially, but that decision had been made long before he was in that office; in national emergencies all high-ranking officials are brought to undisclosed locations. Since she worked for the government now, Jordan decided to ask Agent Barrett about why the U.S. had been so overwhelmed on 9/11.

"We had limited imagination when it came to terror on our own soil. Most of what we saw in foreign countries was a bus, a nightclub, an embassy building blown up by a suicide bomber. Using a commercial jet as a weapon on such a big target was inconceivable-and to take the buildings down? Unbelievable," Agent Barrett explained to Jordan.

Jordan then asked a question she hoped would be answered truthfully. "Agent Barrett," Jordan inquired carefully, "why was the scenario of commercial jets being flown into buildings as weapons inconceivable when the government knew about it in advance?"

"Jordan," Agent Barrett said wryly, "what you see in the tabloids about a 9/11 conspiracy perpetrated by our own government is just plain nonsense."

"Sir, I don't read the tabloids. In 1995 my husband, my children and I were living abroad, in the Netherlands. My husband was in the Army then. They called all the family members to the base, with all their important documents for a three-day exercise. On the first day, they sat us all down and told us there had been a credible threat to take several cross commercial planes hostage and fly them into soft U.S. targets such as public buildings, bridges, the White House, and U.S. interests abroad. We went through a mock evacuation.

They wanted to be able to evacuate hundreds of family members onto military planes within a few hours. The experience was exhausting. We went from station to station where someone official was checking everything from our I.D.s, our shot records, and fingerprints to our passports. It was scary to say the least. I would say that constitutes the U.S. government knowing this kind of large scale attack was conceivable."

Agent Barrett got up, closed the door and addressed Jordan in a more respectful tone. "Jordan, you're right. Yes, we should have known. Although the enemy was making plans, the government really didn't think the terrorists could pull it off, especially after U.S. officials heard about it and took what they *thought* were measured preparations. When nothing happened, they believed it was all hype. Even better, they thought they scared them off. They were wrong, we were wrong- we just didn't let our imaginations run far enough."

Jordan said matter of factly, "Agent Barrett, that is exactly what I thought probably happened. No offense, sir, but the U.S. government is so mired in red tape and inefficiency, it's a wonder you can even find your own offices."

Agent Barrett laughed and said, "Jordan you're right! By the way, this is a good time to tell you something. First, it's just 'Barrett'- forget addressing me as 'Agent' every time you talk to me. Second, you're going to hear things around here that you don't have the clearance to know. I trust you or you wouldn't be here, but for both our sakes, keep this shit to yourself, OK?"

Barrett patted Jordan on the shoulder and she went back to studying the COOP document.

After reading it, she realized if there were an emergency at home, no one would know what to do.

Jordan decided to design a home emergency plan that everyone could be part of.

The following week, Jordan was introduced to Agent Briscoe, the first agent to assign her a duty. Agent Briscoe went to the supply room and retrieved a cart. Jordan watched curiously as he took some papers from a giant stack that was sitting on his windowsill. Eventually the entire stack was moved to the cart.

Jordan said jokingly, "Wow, cleaned out your desk?"

"No," Agent Briscoe said. "These are Intel leads that Homeland Security has received and they need to be processed."

"Ohhhh kaaay, sure thing" Jordan said in a hesitant voice, all the while thinking, *OMG!*

Jordan learned that each piece of Intel had to be divided by regional offices.

Apparently, only when Agent Briscoe occasionally had a few moments would he take one or two leads from the pile and process them. Jordan noticed that some of the Intel was nearly two years old. About a third of them were rather benign, just a report of an illegal alien living in the neighborhood. Barrett had explained to her that illegal aliens not involved with suspicious or criminal activity were ignored. That was their official policy. It contradicted the drum-beating protest groups that would gather outside their building each week. They accused the agency of racism by deporting hardworking illegal immigrant families.

Jordan asked Barrett about it. "Why don't you just set the public straight?"

"How many leads have you processed already?"

"Maybe three thousand?" Jordan estimated.

"Who are the informants?" Barrett inquired.

Jordan answered without hesitation, "Someone from their own life or their own community."

"You are observant, Jordan. Do you think the media would be able to get that point across, would they even try?

We have even had them come in here. Agent Perry from Counterfeit was working the front desk last month when a teenaged girl came in. She said she wanted to report her mother as an illegal alien from Columbia and have her deported. Agent Perry asked why. The girl said her mother was trying to ruin her life by forbidding her to see her boyfriend. Agent Perry told the girl 'Sweetie, if your mother is deported, you'd be deported, too.' The girl stomped her foot angrily and then left. If we wanted to gather up all illegals wouldn't we have detained her? At the time, criminal involvement in major international crimes was the standard for apprehension and deportation. Now our official policy has changed. Having so many unknowns and foreign nationals in this country is a serious national security risk, because those bent on destruction can obtain a valid passport from any country that hates America. It's now a global coalition of terror and criminal enterprises, and, remember..."

"Yes, yes, keep this shit to myself," Jordan said with a smile mixed with concern as she went back to her desk.

The Intel really gave Jordan some serious concern. There was Intel on illegals that were facilitating sex trafficking, drug trafficking and slavery cartels that usually sold women and children for domestics. Jordan also noticed when she would file closed cases of these crimes that they followed a certain pattern. The sale of people, whether for sex or slavery, was international, but within cultural groups. The Chinese sold slaves to

Chinese, Indians sold to Indians, Somalis to Somalis all around the world and likewise for other cultural identities. This made sense to Jordan. Within your own culture you know who you can exploit and who are the exploiters. Marketing and sales across cultures is difficult. What *was* a cross-cultural endeavor was the conglomerate or cartel that developed and controlled these industries.

Barrett told Jordan, "What used to be very fragmented operations around the world selling women, children or drugs on the black market cautiously has now moved into the 21st century. Trafficking is just that- shipping. It's all logistics, and success is based on organization, knowledge and cooperation. These fragmented groups realized their potential for coordinating. They are all partners in transnational crime. The terror groups are the traffickers, the drug runners are the terrorists. Combining their forces, using each other's strengths against the law enforcement agencies of the world, has given them centralization and almost absolute power across the globe. Our ability to police a centralized organization is like battling another super power."

These were the kind of issues Jordan was promised this task force would work on. After several weeks Jordan was still working on processing the Intel and filing closed cases. She decided to go to Agent Briscoe with her concerns of the serious activities reported in the leads, hoping there would be a faster way to get an agent into the field to handle the situation.

"Sir, are these the only leads, the only intelligence this task force receives to do its job?"

"Yes."

"Sir, some of these leads are two years old!"

"We know, Jordan," continued Agent Barrett. "We have very limited staff, limited resources. Last year we were only able to apprehend four hundred thousand serious criminal aliens and deport them."

"Sir, aren't there something like twelve million illegals in this country?"

"In truth, Jordan, there are about twenty million, It's a serious situation. We estimate that about ninety-five percent of the illegals are not criminally involved, just hard workers who want a better life for their families. Our new policy is to apprehend *every* illegal, but honestly, we just can't do it. We first try to target the ones we know are into the organized crime which given the percentages we are still looking at approximately one million criminal aliens."

"You were only able to catch and deport four hundred thousand? That's only about forty percent!"

"You see now how this translates into a serious national security issue?" Barrett said, with a slight nod of his head.

"Sir, some of the Intel I read states those criminals you already deported are back in the same neighborhoods they were captured in, within weeks."

Barrett looked at Jordan discouragingly. "I know... I know... And this shit-"

Jordan interrupted, "Stays between us, got it sir."

Weeks had gone by and Jordan was still analyzing Intel. The work was rewarding, but she felt odd going home at night when the next piece of Intel could be a potential threat to national security. Jordan felt great about being able to earn a paycheck which meant so much to her family.

"Leonard, I've told you all about the emergency preparedness training at work? It's serious training too, everything from long term water and food storage to being able to use a scalpel for onsite emergency surgery. I could actually take out your appendix right now."

"Uh, no, that won't be necessary Doctor. However, I do feel some pain right here in my heart," Leonard said seductively.

"Oh, really." Jordan played along. "I'll just have to investigate."

Jordan felt grateful about the training because she never realized how unprepared she was. She remembered watching the coverage of Hurricane Katrina and saying to Leonard, "I never want to be in the position where I have to wait on someone else to provide water to my children." She had thought the answer was just to leave when the authorities tell you to leave, but that was only part of it. You also had to have a plan of action. On Monday evenings (when there was nothing on TV) she would line up the boys from Thomas down to Seth and give each one something to carry, store, and log into the inventory.

First, everyone had a GOOD ("Get Out of Dodge") Bag. It contained such things as a NOAA radio that had battery, solar, and crank power and several methods to obtain potable water. Jordan also put together bags for medical supplies, tools, shelter, sanitary concerns, and even bags for the pets. Jordan also planned for "sheltering in place,"which stocked the house with water, food and supplies for everyone for six months. There was also stored water and a small ER kit in the car.

***

It was the holidays and they had all just arrived at Lillian's to celebrate. The boys headed to the garage with Roland for a jam session and of course Lillian was huffing and puffing about it. They could hear Carrie and the girls arguing downstairs in their room.

That night the boys were all going to a local pub named 'Toad's Place' to see their favorite up and coming death metal band, '*Cyperna.*' Seth stayed home with all the other adults, but spent the most of the time with Leonard and Ed in the basement work shop while they worked on making a bamboo chair.

Jordan and the girls spent the evening in the living room in front of the fireplace discussing their latest book choice for their own home grown book club. Lillian was into romance novels and had suggested the newest book by Suzanne Brockmann: '*Hot Pursuit.*' The author was one of Jordan's childhood friends. Jordan had never been a romance novel enthusiast, but discussing romance with a room full of women turned out to be wickedly fun. Anne was having fun too, but truth be told she had wanted to go to the concert.

Late Sunday evening Leonard and Jordan were in bed going over the events of the weekend. The topic changed to the Monday morning return to work.

"I told you that since I've been working, I've been spending a lot of time in advanced survival training. It's not like we would be suddenly thrust into a situation like that, but I just didn't know how serious being prepared could be."

"Do you know I think you are the most remarkable woman in the world? Even though you didn't eat your green beans or drink your milk when you were growing up, you still are remarkable. Short, but remarkable," Leonard said.

"Leonard, you really don't know any other women." Jordan pointed out.

"I don't need to, I just know," Leonard said with confidence.

Jordan was right: Leonard was a home body, perfectly content to spend all of his free time with her and the family. Jordan smiled, and they kissed as they laid back onto the bed.

***

Jordan was back at work the next morning by seven o'clock, unlike most of her coworkers. She was at work on the leads when Barrett came in with a boisterous, "Good morning Jordan! Are you ready for something new and exciting?"

"As always."

"The Department is sending about fifty rookies out to northern Michigan for a survival training course, and you're on the list! Uh, you did say you could travel, right? This is an opportunity you wouldn't want to miss!"

"Yes, sir. I am available for any training the agency wants me to have. I do have an odd question though-can I bring somebody?"

"Well, it is an agency activity, but if you mean Leonard, I could arrange that."

"All I have to do is let Leonard know the details so he could put in for leave."

That night at home Leonard seemed very excited about the trip and told Jordan he was approved for leave with no problem. For the next few weeks they were busy with work and family like usual, with the additional stress of arranging for their time away. The house was full of adults, but sometimes you had to spell things out for the boys. Each person had to be assigned specific responsibilities or they'd always think someone else took care of it. Jordan knew that Thomas was the most responsible, so she put him in charge during their absence.

The day of their departure arrived. Leonard and Jordan took the train to the federal building in the city. The supplies and the people filled up two luxury travel buses, and by eleven o'clock they were on their way to the wilderness in northern Michigan.

The tree branches hung down like partially closed umbrellas, heavy with freshly fallen snow. The buses were met by a crowd of instructors wearing snow camouflage and carrying M4 assault rifles. The trainees thought that after this long, grueling ride they would be shown to their cabins to shower, eat and rest before training began in the morning, but they stood there in awkward silence. As they started to gather their bags from the cargo area a piercing siren went off. They were herded across the compound, leaving most of their possessions on the ground.

"Move it! Move it! Move it!" the instructors bellowed, sounding more like drill sergeants than teachers. The trainees ran until they got to an open metal hatch guarded on both sides by the camouflaged "soldiers" still barking orders, now steering them to go down the staircase that led underground. As they gathered in a large, dark room at the end of a long tunnel the instructors stood at the doorway until their commander stepped front and center.

"If we hadn't corralled you, you would all now be dead! A dirty nuke was just deployed 10 clicks from our current location. You had twenty minutes to get underground to safety. Between your bungling over your belongings, not moving when we said to move and your general lack of seriousness, you are dead and you have killed many of my men. If this had been an actual attack, I assure you my men would be in here and you would be out there! While you are here, you will be cold, you will be hungry, you will be wet, you will be tired, and you will be pushed to the limit both physically and mentally. When you leave here, you will know exactly what to do, not if, but *when* this occurs, possibly in your own city! You will learn to think quickly or you will die!"

August 2010

Jordan had been at her job with the Department of Homeland Security for nearly eight months. She had already completed the backlog of leads. Since Jordan was now only spending about two hours a day processing Intel, Barrett had given her other assignments to work on.

A few months ago he had asked her to put together an ethnographic assessment of the Tribes of Yemen. Where that report went and what it was used for Jordan never found out, but she hoped it was helpful. Then a few weeks later he asked Jordan to put together an official report summarizing all the training she had received so far. A week earlier, he had asked Jordan to put together an original Disaster Response Plan for a fictitious corporation with more than two hundred employees in the heart of a major American city. Jordan figured she was being evaluated on her knowledge, but never heard anything after she turned it over to Barrett.

There were times when Barrett would have Jordan sit at his assistant's desk to fill in for her while she was on an errand. Often when this would happen, other agents would show up in his office to discuss operations. His assistant would return afterwards. As Jordan left, Barrett would give her a nod.

"Jordan," he would say, "you and Leonard only, okay?"

"Yes, sir, shit kept," Jordan would reply as she scurried out. Jordan named these incidents 'sit-ins.'

***

It was Thursday night and Jordan and Leonard were getting into bed.

"Leonard, some of the information I've heard at work can be quite disturbing," Jordan said, concerned.

"I know. If you hadn't been the one who told me about such things I would have dismissed it already as crazy."

"Today I had another one of my 'sit-ins' with Barrett. Of course I am not in the meeting, I am at his assistant's desk, but it's really inside his office with only a mobile six-foot wall in between. The cast of agency VIPs that come in and out of there is mind boggling and I don't think they know I'm there- well, at least they act like I'm invisible. Anyway, they were discussing how the federal network had been hacked by China twice in the past six months. It was penetrated by Chinese high school students, during class, with their teacher, and it was sanctioned by the Chinese government and their version of the CIA, the MSS. They penetrated the firewalls and accessed classified materials. Our government didn't make a formal complaint against China because we owe them so much money!"

"Well, I don't get to hear top secret discussions or read classified Intel, but some of the things I'm seeing lately don't seem to make much sense," Leonard offered. "In the past few months we've seized several small 'Go Fasts' off the coast. They contained mostly drug bales and runners. Typical, right? But the runners were odd. There were about four runners in each boat and they all had Venezuelan, Ecuadorian or Colombian passports. I spoke to some of these guys- they were supposed to be speaking Spanish, but it didn't sound right. GM3 Ortiz is originally from Mexico and he agreed with me. We both told GM1 Harris something wasn't right, but he blew it off. The next time we catch one, I should have you come down to the station before

CBP picks them up so you can observe them. Being an anthropologist, I know you have some knowledge of language and physical appearance."

"Well, anthropological linguistics is a specialized field within anthropology. We only touched on linguistics. I could, in a very general sense, analyze his physical appearance and speech, but I couldn't be accurate. You should really call in an expert," Jordan said hesitantly.

"I've seen you guess where foreigners are from by just listening to them. We know you were right because we always asked them afterwards. Why couldn't you do that here?"

"Because that's a game! It's fun to do that! I can do that only because of all the languages I took in school, not because of the little bit I have learned about linguistics," Jordan protested.

"Maybe it's a combination of the two. Besides, no one is asking for you to do this officially. If you said something to WO4 Feinstein that these runners' origins are fishy, he may take you seriously enough to call in an expert or make a suggestion higher up the chain."

"That sounds reasonable... As long as you won't make me out to be some sort of expert- because I'm not." Jordan's smile belied her seriousness.

"You are the smartest person I know, you know that?"

"Yes, yes, I know you think that, but I don't agree," Jordan teased.

"Well, my opinion is all that matters," Leonard said as he embraced her.

***

At 4:00 a.m. Jordan woke up to the sound of giggling and went to investigate. She could see that all the lights were on downstairs. There was definitely someone down there giggling and it didn't sound like an adult. It brought back such memories. Marshal was her mischievous one and used to wake her up during the night with all sorts of mayhem. She followed the laughter down the stairs when Seth went sliding past her covered in chocolate.

"OMG!" she whispered. "We have another Marshal on our hands."

Seth had taken a five-gallon drum of chocolate frozen yogurt out of the freezer, turned it upside down on the floor near the front door until it plopped out of the container and was sliding in it from the front door all the way to the back door. There was chocolate on the walls, the ceiling, the furniture, the curtains and of course, Seth! Jordan put her hand over her mouth and laughed ever so slightly, which is when Seth turned around and saw her. He stood up, and just stared at her. Jordan tried to compose herself and put on a serious face.

"Seth, what are you doing? Were you dreaming of this and you just had to wake up and try it?"

"Yep!" Seth said, as if that explained it all.

"What a mess," Jordan said to herself. Then she clapped her hands and ordered, "Okay mister, let's get you cleaned up, back to bed, and the next time your dreams tell you to get up and try something crazy, will you come wake Mema first?"

Seth just shook his head yes. After giving him a bath and putting him back to bed, she went downstairs to clean the chocolate off of everything. Jordan never went back to bed, getting ready for work instead.

It was Friday, the last day of a busy work week and Jordan was looking forward to the family weekend at Lillian's. It was only 7:20 a.m. but Jordan was already at her desk. Her mind was filled with what food they should bring to Lillian's, not to forget their latest book for discussion and yes, she couldn't wait to tell everyone about Seth. She felt kind of bad she would have to tell Thomas that he had the mischievous child and not Marshal.

Barrett interrupted her thoughts with a sudden "Jordan!" He sounded serious. "I need you at my assistant's desk before eight- be there!" Barrett said as he walked away.

Jordan was in place at the assistant's desk by 7:45. At 8:17, several VIPs showed up and sat down in Barrett's office. Jordan didn't know who was saying what, but listened carefully as she typed on the computer distractedly.

"Do they really have him secured?"

"Yes, they are bringing him here next Thursday."

"This is unbelievable. With all our capabilities, we wouldn't even come close to what this guy could give us."

"I know, but more importantly, they know. We have to keep him safe. I mean safer than safe. Do you all understand? We have less than a week to come up with a proposal to keep him secure. This is witness protection on steroids, no mistakes! Put together your own proposals and give them to me by Monday at ten. I'll choose what I think is the most comprehensive plan."

The group moved with purpose out of Barrett's office and left the floor. Jordan just sat there wondering what the hell was going on. She saw the assistant come into the unit so she stood up to go, but looked over to Barrett's desk first.

He looked up at Jordan very seriously and said, "al Qaeda."

"Major shit," Jordan said trying hard not to be funny, because it didn't seem appropriate.

"Yeah," Barrett said with an apprehensive smile.

Jordan didn't ask any questions and went back to her work. Barrett came to Jordan's desk shortly after lunch and asked her if she had another copy of her training report.

"Did you outline exactly the training you received in Michigan?" he asked.

"Yes, sir. Wilderness survival, nuclear attack survival methods, info on NEST, DCRF and CBRN/CBIRF protocol. The report is written in detail, sir."

Instead of explaining himself, Barrett just walked away, leaving Jordan mystified.

On her way back from the city, she tried to put the thoughts of that day out of her head. It was too much to get her head around without knowing very much.

They arrived at Lillian's house by 9:00 in the evening and settled in. Ed came up to Jordan's bedroom and asked Leonard to come to the porch and talk with him. Jordan went downstairs and could hear that the boys were already in the garage with Roland playing music. She walked past the study when she heard a faint sniffle, so she opened the door. Carrie was sitting in there all by herself and it looked like she had been crying.

"Hey, what's wrong?" Jordan inquired.

"Oh, nothing Jordan, just the same old crap. The girls can't find a job that they would enjoy. I told them they had to start working regardless if they enjoyed it or not if they ever wanted to go back to school. They weren't too happy with me. Of course Roland 'understands them' and only agrees with me in private," Carrie said bitterly.

Jordan knew that Roland didn't understand the damage he was doing by coddling the girls and by not setting them straight. All he cared about was how good it felt for the girls to like him over Carrie.

"He needs a good kick in the head, don't you think?" Jordan joked. She gave her sister a hug and left the room.

Jordan walked down the hallway into the empty living room. She could hear Leonard and Ed talking on the porch right outside the window. She wondered where everyone else was. Jordan went into the kitchen to marinate the chicken for tomorrow's BBQ. When she finished, she went into the garage and there was everyone else listening to the boys play, even Lillian.

The boys had set up an odd collection of seats to look like a concert hall. Lillian was in the back row of seats with this look on her face like she was laying an egg. Jordan guessed she was trying to look happy. Anne was sitting in the front row clapping even though the claps didn't match the heavy guitar rift or the creepy chorus Thomas was growling into the mic. The kids were all in their own little mosh pit down in front. Jordan sat down next to Lillian and started yelling and cheering like she and Leonard used to do at a Pat Benatar or a Guns N' Roses concert. Ed and Leonard finally came in. Ed sat down with Lillian and was happy to see that she was making an effort. Leonard took his place with Jordan and they both let loose like a couple of teenagers.

"You know you look like Cousin It when you wear your hair down, right?" Leonard said, teasing Jordan not only about her height, but also about her long hair.

"Yeah, but you love it."

"Yes, yes I do," Leonard said as he picked up Jordan and spun her around.

***

"Well, what's the big story? I know you've had something on your mind all day, so out with it!" Leonard exclaimed.

"It's not good news, sweetie. I had another 'sit in' with Barrett. There was a serious discussion about bringing some informant here next week. I've never seen them this excessively concerned with an informant's security. When the VIPs left, Barrett had this look on his face, it was a mixture of fear and anxiety, and all he could say to me was 'al Qaeda.' I don't know what to make of it. My only guess is that they have a defector from the inner circle. Maybe he has information on a future attack? I just wish that the world would grow up and learn how to love and care for everyone, even if they are different, you know, like John Lennon's song, 'Imagine'," Jordan said with conviction.

"Will that ever happen?" Leonard asked.

"No, probably not!" Jordan said realistically. They gave each other a kiss as they lay back on the bed.

***

On Saturday afternoon, Roland and the boys were back in the garage playing music, and since it was warm, they had the door open. Jordan relaxed on the back porch as Ed and some of the others were by the pond fishing, talking about crime and war. She watched as Megan and Janice took Ashley into the garden to pick tomatoes and cucumbers for lunch. The fish that was caught that morning was added to the chicken, burgers and hotdogs. During lunch Jordan spoke up.

"Hey, Thomas." Everyone turned toward Jordan to listen.

"I believe you have a 'Marshal'!" she said as she continued to tell Thomas and the whole family about Seth's escapades of Thursday night.

Anne just burst out laughing. Everyone knew they had to keep a closer eye on Seth. Thomas wasn't too happy, having already experienced the original. He had also hoped that Marshal himself would have a son just like him.

It was late in the evening. Wesley and Jay were having a heated discussion about the upcoming NFL season as they walked past the girls on the porch on their way to the garage. The girls were on the back porch to have their discussion about the new Brockmann book, *Infamous.* Carrie and the girls were getting along. Reading these books had allowed them to relax and be silly together. It was comforting.

"The boys told me about the drills and the 'GOOD Bags' you put together? It sounds like you're preparing for Armageddon or something," Megan said. Lillian and Anne laughed. They had never told Jordan what they thought of her emergency plans.

"We just think it's kinda silly- like Megan said, it sounds like you're one of those nuts who builds a bunker underground," Lillian said with Anne agreeing with her.

"Really, is that what you think?" Jordan asked, not too surprised. Lillian and Anne were from a different age, and to them, the government and the community would always be on top of things. "No, I am not building a bunker, this is part of my job. They want us to be the ones in our families that are ready for any foreseeable disastrous event," Jordan explained. Megan moved closer to Jordan and told her she didn't think she was nuts. She really wanted to know more and they spent some time together discussing it.

***

The following Thursday, everything was abuzz at work with the rumors flying around that a defector from al Qaeda was arriving. Security was tight at the federal building that day and one of the elevators was earmarked for their unit only. It was inaccessible without a code. Barrett came over to Jordan's desk and told her he transferred his assistant, so she was going to permanently "sit in."

Several immigrations officers brought the man to Barrett's office, and as he walked past Jordan's new desk, she was very surprised and confused. Barrett walked in and stopped in front of Jordan.

"Sir, that man is Chinese!" Jordan said, surprised.

"I know, Jordan, you need to pay attention to a whole pile of shit this week, understand?" Barrett said urgently. Jordan decided to hang up her digital recorder on the corner of the partition between their desks.

His name was Zhao Minsheng and he was Chinese Intelligence. The Ministry of State Security (MSS) was a complex agency with divisions called bureaus. Zhao was one of two assistant directors. He was in charge of the 2nd (Foreign Affairs), 6th (Counter Intelligence), 8th (Research) and 9th (Anti-Defection & Counter Surveillance) Bureaus. He had been an agent for twenty-two years. He told Barrett that there was another agent also defecting, but had not heard from him since they were separated in Belarus. His name was Sun Li and had been one of the top agents working for him. Zhao said he had always been a firm believer in the People's Republic of China. They had worked together to create a strong and prosperous country for the people.

"My parents, who were farmers, named me Minsheng. It means 'voice of the people.' They were very loyal. I have always been loyal, but corruption has slithered in, for it is no longer the people building a strong home together, but rather government using the people to make itself more politically powerful and rich," Zhao said sadly. "Trying to destroy and conquer other countries and dominate the world is beyond the people's peaceful aspirations."

The first Intel he shared with them was how his government, working through the intelligence agency, had joined a human trafficking ring operating throughout the former eastern bloc countries. This criminal organization was trafficking women from Poland, Romania, Hungary and Czechoslovakia when they decided to expand their operations into Russia, the Ukraine, Bulgaria and Moldova in the mid to late 90s. They had well-established routes where the authorities were just bribed to look the other way. About a decade ago they began to move into Asia. They were shipping girls from Uzbekistan, Kazakhstan, Kyrgyzstan and Georgia mostly for sex, but some for domestic servitude.

"That is when our government first met with them. At first it was justified by saying it was a way for our government to operate a more extensive spy enterprise. They would mix female operatives with the young girls that we kidnapped from their families. They were given to the traffickers who would then smuggle them into the western countries like Germany, the U.K., Canada and the United States. The kidnapped girls were sold to other Chinese who lived in these countries. The undercover agents though were delivered to other operatives. It turned out to be the most efficient way to get operatives into another country and our government started to make a considerable amount of money. We already had a few intelligence operatives living in the

U.S. undetected for fifteen years, but since 2001 when we began working with the traffickers, we have deployed thousands. One mission our operatives engage in is to increase the legitimate population of Chinese in the states. We have many Chinese-American lawyers that work with us. We have these operatives travel around the U.S. to meet with large groups of immigrants. We tell them what to say on the asylum paperwork and how to answer an investigator's questions. Even though these applications are identical, and the answers given to investigators are virtually word for word, they are never denied. It is very big business. These immigrants are indebted to our government for this opportunity," Zhao explained precisely. "I have the names and aliases of some of our agents that are here in the U.S."

***

Barrett acted upon the list Zhao gave him and put together a team for the local targets. They raided several homes, restaurants and retail locations and arrested several MSS Agents. In the process they were left holding about three hundred slaves just from the immediate area. They were also able to find documentation about who had purchased some the kidnapped girls. Other jurisdictions did just as well. Jordan was astonished.

"How could there be slaves in the U.S.?" she asked Barrett.

"It's just the tip of the iceberg, Jordan. There are thousands upon thousands. There are tunnels that cross over our northern border from Canada that have permanent walls and electricity. According to Zhao, some of these slaves don't even know where they are. They are kept in Chinese homes behind closed doors and fences. One woman escaped. She was running and screaming for her life and when she got to the public road do you know what she saw? American children playing in their yards and neighbors tending to their lawn."

Zhao told Barrett that he was laying the groundwork so he would be able to understand the coming threat. He explained that since there were so many conspirators around the globe invested and making millions, they could take their time in planning a detailed attack. Cooperation was the key. The criminal underworld- from Mexican drug cartels to Eastern bloc mobs- were joining forces with terrorist organizations such as the Tamil Tigers and al Qaeda, as well as Afghan warlords, failed African states, and rogue states like Iran and North Korea. The criminal and evil were becoming a transnational criminal united force against the good in every country.

"This coalition is planning a multilayered attack which includes a nuclear strike," said Zhao seriously.

Barrett and Jordan stopped for a moment and looked at each other as if to say, "This shit is going to hit the fan." Barrett was right, if Zhao had Intel on future plans to hit the U.S., all hell was going to break loose. Just then, a few other agents entered the room and whispered to Barrett. Barrett got up and called for the security detail assigned to Zhao.

"Take Zhao to the safe house."

Just then, Special Agent in Charge Johnson arrived at Barrett's office along with half a dozen other agents Jordan had never met before.

"The MSS agents previously captured have apparently all hanged themselves in prison. Each of them was being held in separate locations, in isolation-how on earth could they have coordinated to kill themselves on the same day?" Johnson mused.

Jordan remembered something Zhao had said earlier, scribbled it on a piece of paper and quietly handed it to Barrett. The note said, *Remember, they possibly have American citizen Chinese operatives working as attorneys- they would have had access to their clients.* Barrett suggested this as a way this action was coordinated.

Johnson said, "If the attorneys are also operatives then MSS directed actions were still being implemented. Those lawyers were in and out of this building during the original interrogations of those MSS agents, so there is a possibility they saw Zhao, which means his location has been compromised. Contact the security detail and tell them to turn around and bring Zhao back here. We need to design a new protection plan."

Zhao was back in Barrett's office within an hour, sitting across from Jordan's desk while the agents came up with a new plan. He informed them they had more than a year before the attacks were to take place, so he was flown by helicopter that afternoon to Dover Air Force Base in Maryland. It was decided it was too dangerous for Zhao ever to be recognized again, so they arranged for a vetted plastic surgeon to change Zhao's face completely. The surgery and recuperation took place at the 436th Medical Operations Squadron.

Zhao was back in Barrett's office two weeks later. He walked in wearing a Fedora and sunglasses. He looked tired, his face still swollen, and he certainly didn't look like he used to, but it was him. There were new agents assigned to his security detail and he had yet another new identity, new safe house location and instructions to never contact anyone he knew, not even his family.

Zhao spent the next few weeks detailing the coming threats against the U.S. It was not going to take place on 9/11. Every year security was tight around this day of remembrance, but according to Zhao, the coalition wanted multiple days of mourning for their enemies. Attacking on 9/11 again only gives them the same day to mourn.

"It's like an American being born on Christmas Day, you feel cheated." Zhao said trying to use an analogy that they would understand. He continued, "I will first give you a general outline and then go into detail. They want to self fulfill doomsday prophecies. They believe it will give their cause legitimacy if it is tied in with an ancient prophecy, as if it were meant to be. They do not believe in the prophecy itself, rather they want to use the fear associated with it to their advantage. The top members of the factions within this coalition meet every month in Australia to plan the details of this event. They will begin on December 21, 2012. There will be seven consecutive days of attacks, with nineteen missions each day. Each mission consists of seven strikes. There were plans to deploy a ten kiloton nuclear weapon each of the seven days, but when I left, they had only acquired enough fissile material to create three of them."

He would give more details on the plans for this major attack, but in the meantime, agencies knew where to direct their focus on intelligence gathering. Barrett said it would take months to analyze all the Intel Zhao was giving them. They needed him, especially in counter intelligence efforts, if they had any hope of stopping this evil plan.

The U.S. intelligence community believed that a single ten kiloton nuclear weapon deployed in the U.S. was the number one, most likely attack scenario to the American homeland. Their efforts around the world capturing insurgents in the act of buying fissile material had been so successful that some believed that a rogue nuclear weapon would never come to fruition. Barrett and Jordan felt differently.

***

By the time Jordan got home Friday night she was exhausted mentally and emotionally. She had talked to Leonard every night about what was being revealed.

"Sweetie, you grow up in America, the 'land of the free and home of the brave' and then you have your eyes opened to this corruption that slithers around just under the veneer of the civilized. There are parts of the world that are so embroiled in venality and turmoil that... it's like they want company. Subversive elements and operations are taking place because they are riding in on the coattails of our vices, indifference and ignorance. The drugs, the illegals, the sex slaves, the debt, and God I hate to say it, even the oil," Jordan explained. Leonard sat there in bed staring at her. It was quiet for several long moments until Leonard broke the silence.

"WOW! Um ... you sound like a preacher or a politician or something. I don't mean that in a negative way really, it's just that you are into this deeply. I don't know whether to be impressed or worried, especially from someone who didn't eat her green beans or drink her milk when she was growing up," Leonard said, teasing Jordan about her height again.

"I'm sorry, Leonard, it's a lot to take in," Jordan said realizing how animated she had become.

"Hey, I'll bet you this kind of stuff has been going on for decades. We shouldn't be shocked- immoral activities have always tried to trump decency. I mean, can you imagine all the behind closed doors dealings that went on during the Cold War?

"You're right, I guess the world is full of secrets and facades. We're just getting to peek behind the curtain and it makes us uneasy. Trouble may be lurking, but I don't want it to visit our house," Jordan said cautiously.

Leonard held Jordan tightly and turned off the light. "I love it when you're intense, especially with me," Leonard said teasingly.

***

It was Monday, time for work again after what seemed to be a very quick weekend at Lillian's. She listened as Zhao went into detail about how his country, al Qaeda, and the other malicious factions around the world grew into an evil coalition. It was a who's who of evil which included such members as corrupt government officials in Australia, anti-western states like Iran, North Korea and Venezuela, failed states such as Somalia and the Congo, drug cartels from Mexico and Colombia, crime syndicates from Russia, Belarus and Moldova, the high tech, soon to be world power, China and of course the Muslim radical terrorist group of the decade: al Qaeda. It even included a few homegrown crazies that were big time wannabes. It was fast becoming a culture of its own- a radicalized culture of hatred, perversion and greed. The Middle East had been a harbinger of terror for a long time, but al Qaeda had finally taken the lead as the centralizing enterprise of this coalition. They had spent years campaigning outside their comfort zone to syndicates around the world with the idea, "The enemy of my enemy is my friend." They felt this could work toward their advantage in a monumental way. When these leaders got together, they would posture that they would be the opposing coalition force that could finally take down their common enemy: the United States. The recruiting of insurgents and operatives for this international terror league had even gone digital, with its own website and marketing videos. It didn't matter that all their motives were different, they all wanted to change the face of the world to their advantage.

One of the many unique cooperative missions they had going was to send serious operatives to Venezuela or Australia. They received training in these countries to speak Spanish or English as a native speaker and learn the culture. Then these countries would give these terrorists, some already on watch lists, legitimate birth certificates and passports from their countries. Now, they could obtain visas and travel to the United States in first class. Most Americans could not tell the physical difference between most foreign nationals and could not decipher accents. When their visas expired, they blended in with the rest of the illegals that, even when reported, were never pursued.

Zhao was laying out more details each day about this transnational criminal coalition, how it was structured and operated, but most importantly he continued detailing everything he knew about plans for future attacks against the United States. One day after Zhao was finished for the day and the security detail was on its way to pick him up, he walked by Jordan's desk and stopped. Jordan looked up at Zhao.

"Barrett is concerned about you and your family," he said. Then he continued very deliberately, "you know, I have always wanted to buy vacation property in your northern Maine."

Jordan was just puzzled as he continued to look at her as he walked away. Barrett came back to the office thirty minutes later, sat down at his desk, then looked over to Jordan.

"Very serious shit, sir," Jordan said cautiously.

"Very, very serious, as serious as that cow in Chicago," Barrett said.

"Wh ... whaaat cow sir?"

"The cow, in the barn, she wanted to burn the barn down, she didn't like Chicago or something," Barrett said, fumbling over his words.

"Ohhh, Mrs. O'Leary's cow. Sir, I think that was an accident. The cow didn't premeditate arson," Jordan said trying to figure out if Barrett was attempting a joke to lighten the mood or if he just sucked at analogies.

"The point is it spread and did massive damage for such a mindless single act," said Barrett. He said nothing for several minutes, lost in thought, and then looked up at Jordan and said, "You know you're short."

March 2011

One Monday Leonard called Jordan at work and told her that they had captured another boat with suspicious persons on board and wanted her to stop there after work. Leonard and Ortiz approached GM1 Harris again after they brought the boat and its passengers back to the station. He agreed to let Jordan observe the prisoners.

Jordan had spent some time over the past few months familiarizing herself with the finer points of linguistics, especially after what she had learned from Zhao about terrorists masking as legitimate travelers. She went back to her Anthropology professors for help, especially the Anthropological Linguists. They had helped her become a bit more familiar deciphering an accent. She felt confident she could at least be certain of where they *weren't* from, but beyond that, Professor Bicks told her he would come and help her if she needed it.

Jordan arrived at Leonard's station and met with GM1 Harris. He wasn't convinced there was a problem, but was a little more concerned than the first few times Leonard and Ortiz had approached him. Jordan sat down near the holding cell and just watched and listened. She wanted to be sure. Within a few minutes she knew at least physically these men were not native to Honduras, where their passports were from. She was also sure that Spanish was not their native tongue. However, there was always the possibility that these men's parents or grandparents had been immigrants to Honduras, so she really needed to listen to them speak for a while. Jordan went with Leonard and Ortiz to see GM1 Harris.

"Sir, those men are not from Honduras, and they are not from South or Central America, I'm certain. As far as where they *are* from, maybe Yemen?"

GM1 Harris looked sick. Maybe he realized the possibility that several operatives were just deported back to South America instead of being detained because of his stubbornness. He knew he had to make it right, so he arranged for Jordan, Leonard and Ortiz to see Warrant Officer Feinstein.

WO4 Feinstein found Jordan credible and believed they had a serious situation on their hands. He immediately ordered additional security on the men being held, arranged for Professor Bicks to observe the men, and contacted the First District Command in Boston. A joint meeting was set up for everyone involved to meet with First District Commander Godson and Vice Admiral Thakur of the Atlantic Command. Jordan had also contacted Barrett and told him everything. Barrett invited himself to the meeting and on a bright and beautiful Wednesday morning they all flew on an Air Force C130 out of Gabreski Air field on Long Island.

As they got on the plane Jordan remarked about the first step on the stairs being ridiculously high.

"That's because you didn't eat your green beans and drink your milk when you were growing up," Leonard said with a smile.

They landed at Hanscom Air Force Base north of Boston. A car was sent to pick them up and drive them to the Coast Guard First District Command.

The meeting started with each person explaining his or her part to the Commander and the Vice Admiral. Professor Bicks was certain these men were from Sana'a, Yemen. Barrett explained they had Intel on an authentic passport operation to facilitate terrorists' entry into the United States. Admiral Thakur and Commander Godson were quite impressed with Leonard, Jordan and Ortiz for having uncovered the risk, even before DHS and Barrett had the Intel. They returned home the next morning.

***

The following Friday night Jordan and her family all left for Lillian's house. The girls were starting on the new Suzanne Brockmann book: *Breaking the Rules.* On Saturday afternoon Jordan took Foster from Chloe so she could go fishing with Marshal. Jordan sat in the living room feeding and rocking Foster until he fell asleep. She didn't see anyone else until Seth came walking past her.

"Sweetie, where you going?" She didn't see anyone with him as he walked into the kitchen. Jordan was more aware than anyone else what mischievous boys could get into, so she got up with Foster still sleeping in her arms and followed him. Seth was standing in front of the refrigerator with the door open, pouring a 44oz. bottle of ketchup on Lillian's cat.

"Seth, don't move. Don't say a word. Be very quiet," Jordan whispered.

That didn't work. Seth started jumping up and down screaming at the top of his lungs for no apparent reason. The cat went running, flinging ketchup everywhere, and Foster woke up crying. She placed Foster in the playpen, still crying, grabbed the cat and put her outside. At that point Wesley, who had been in the back yard talking to Megan and Janice, came inside. He picked up Foster, went onto the back porch and started rocking him again. Jordan caught Seth while the girls started cleaning up.

"Seth, I thought we talked about acting out your silly dreams!" Jordan sighed with a smile.

"You were already awake," Seth replied, as if that made it perfectly all right.

Jordan suddenly remembered she had told Seth to wake her up before acting on his crazy dreams the last time she had to clean up one of his messes.

***

Sunday afternoon they were all having dinner when Jordan asked Lillian if she had followed her instructions for an emergency closet. Lillian just laughed and said she felt there really was no reason for it. Jordan already knew that Lillian, Anne and even Carrie thought it was a silly idea. They had been through this before, but Jordan was getting a vibe from all this uncertainty at work and really wanted them to be a little better prepared than just what supplies were in the house at any given time.

"Mom, most people have enough food on hand for only nine complete meals, no stored water, no batteries and no alternative cooking method. If more people were adequately prepared, the stores wouldn't be depleted right after there was a warning for a hurricane or tornado. You don't always get a warning. I know this is the U.S. and not Port-au-Prince, but you should still plan for more than three days. That's the definition of an emergency- something you don't think will happen, but it happens countless times around the world every year."

"Jordan- GG, your father, and I have been through many tough times and we have always made it just fine," Lillian said, dismissing Jordan.

Megan and Janice took Jordan aside and assured her that they would do it on their own. Jordan was relieved.

Ashley, who was now three years old, came running up to Jordan.

"Mema, up!" she chirped.

Jordan picked Ashley up.

"Gee whiz, sweetie, what do you feed this girl? She's getting so tall!" Jordan asked Candace, who trailed behind the toddler.

"Mom, everyone is tall to you- you're only five feet tall, the size of a fourth grader," Candace said.

"Yeah, yeah, yeah," Jordan said, laughing. "Hey sweetie, where in Maine do you guys have that hunting cabin?"

"It's in Aroostook County, why?"

"Oh, your father and I were just thinking of buying a vacation property up there. We want to be near the Canadian border. Is that where Aroostook County is?" Jordan asked.

"Yeah, it's way up there. It would be wonderful to have some family nearby," Candace said.

Jordan had been thinking of what Zhao said that day about Maine. She had been told to pay attention, but the government had uncovered the plot, so all was well...right?

***

On Sunday evening while they lay in bed together at home, Jordan asked Leonard about buying some land in Maine.

"Well, I have been working for seventeen months now and I have managed to set aside enough money for Wesley to go back to school. He could start this summer and he would probably be finished by December. I took a look at some properties up where Candace and Richard have their cabin and it's quite affordable," Jordan explained.

"It's affordable because not too many people want to live up there," Leonard quipped. "I mean, Homeland

Security has had the details of these plots since August, so they nipped it in the bud, right?"

"Yes... Yes, it would seem so." Jordan hesitated. "There are so many details swimming around in my head from the past few months of listening to Zhao. He has revealed these intricate, sinister plans for undermining the entire U.S. system. How could all that possibly be over? The Chinese want dictatorial communism, al Qaeda wants Taliban interpreted Shari'ah Law and the rest just want to get rich. If there is an election through our democratic system and the majority vote to rescind democracy and install Communism or Shari'ah Law... If you could undermine the voting process with those intentionally placed asylum seekers, combined with the fact that many Americans don't even bother to vote, could it be done? It is so twisted and freaking complicated. It seems that they've figured out every one of our political or moral weaknesses, like the voting..."

"And the drugs," Leonard interrupted.

"Yes, and they are going to exploit them every way they can. You know, this global coalition of transnational crime is so hypocritical. The terrorists are willing to join forces with drug lords, kiddie peddlers, slave traders and even a political competitor: the Communists. It's a lie- men lie! It's power, money, and access to sex. Leonard, I don't think it will ever stop. There are so many factions, rogue regimes and failed states that are a part of this coalition, I don't think uncovering their plans has deterred them in any way. Zhao said they were patient and taking their time to devise a plan that is so monumental, it won't matter if one or two of the strikes are foiled. Their mission is to physically destroy parts of America, collapse the financial infrastructure, kill and hurt as many

Americans as possible and make us unable to conduct our normal lives."

Leonard whispered, "Gloooobal cooooling." Jordan leaned back into his arms.

"You're so silly," she said. Leonard held onto her tightly and turned off the light.

***

That week Zhao continued laying out specific details about the coordinated plans to take down the United States. SAC Johnson was not convinced that any rogue regime or terrorist group had the capability to carry out the kind of strikes Zhao was describing. Barrett tried to explain to Johnson how powerful and massive this evil coalition had become, but Johnson said he didn't believe that so many factions, comprised of so many cultures, could work with each other long enough. Their differences would cause them to turn on each other, and the coalition would implode before they could strike in unison against the United States. Johnson also revealed that he doubted Zhao's credibility, and aired his suspicions that Zhao was just guaranteeing his new lifestyle on the American taxpayer dime. Barrett and Jordan thought Johnson had gone crazy, considering he was the one that had brought Zhao to the agency in the first place and had touted his critical significance.

It had been a frustrating week. Both Barrett and Jordan believed the threat was imminent, credible and even more complicated than even Zhao let on.

December 2011

Just before they descended on Lillian's for the Christmas break, Leonard and Jordan joined Richard and Candace for a two-day trip to their cabin in Aroostook, Maine. They had arranged to look at a wonderful piece of property about twenty minutes from Richard's cabin. It was sixty-five acres that was partially wooded, partially open with a freshwater river that ran through the eastern third of the property. It also had a mid-sized pond at the base of one of the hills. It was perfect. Leonard had decided to take an early retirement benefit, a lump sum payment that he had been offered, to buy the land. It would reduce his future pension by ten percent, but they felt it was worth it.

The boys were all in the garage with Roland playing their music. Wesley had just graduated from college the previous weekend and was particularly happy to be finished. Roland and Carrie had managed to save enough money for Megan to return to school. They announced it at dinner Friday evening and Megan began to cry. Carrie apologetically explained to Janice that she wasn't going to be able to return to school yet. Janice surprised everyone by saying she was willing to wait until Megan was finished. It seemed that the girls were maturing a bit. They had recently been able to find part time jobs and were contributing to the food budget.

The Saturday after Christmas was a good day to catch up on household chores. Jordan went to the laundry room to put her first load of wash into the dryer. Just as she opened the dryer door to throw the laundry in, something shiny caught her eye. She put the wash into a basket and leaned into the dryer to investigate. The dryer was already warm and there was something at the base of the drum. It almost looked like wax, but it turned out to be a puddle of melted butter.

Jordan stood up and yelled, "Seth!"

At Sunday dinner Marshal got everyone's attention and said he had an announcement to make. He said that since he had a family of his own to support, he needed to move on to something more permanent than part time work at a grocery store. He had enlisted in the Army. He was going to be an Explosive Ordnance Disposal (EOD) Specialist. The reaction from the family was a mixture of applause and fear. Jordan and Leonard, who had always encouraged their children, congratulated and praised him for his decision. Privately, they were worried for him and fearful of what might happen if indeed the threats to the U.S. became reality.

"That's the nature of being in the combat forces, there is always an expectation of hostilities," Leonard said, torn between patriotism and fatherhood. "I am proud of him wanting to defend our country, I am proud he has taken on the mantle of the provider, but he is also my son, and I don't want to lose him."

"I can't imagine my baby in war or in some hostile humanitarian situation, which can be just as dangerous! Leonard, you know this is exactly what you did when we got married so young. He's taking after you! Our parents probably felt the same way," Jordan said tearfully.

"It's going to be all right, he's a man now. All we can do is support him and keep him and his family in our prayers always."

They held each other tightly, falling asleep in each other's arms.

***

The following Saturday afternoon was a lazy day sitting on the back porch, which for the winter had been turned into a large sun room. The girls discussed the latest Brockmann publication, a short story called "When Tony Met Adam". Most of the family didn't expect Lillian or Anne to participate, given their generation's cultural view towards homosexuals.

"It's referred to as the gay community now, GG," Megan said to Anne.

Anne came back with a simple "Oh," and they both went about discussing the story as they would any literary work. It seemed that growing maturity and change was not only reserved for the young.

That Sunday at dinner, Jordan and Leonard decided to talk to the whole family about the potential for future attacks against America.

"Everyone, I need to talk to you about something important. I know some of you think it is unnecessary to prepare for any kind emergency greater than a natural disaster such as a hurricane. You feel it is sufficient to stock some extra batteries and canned goods in the garage, expecting that everything will be back to normal in a few days. I can't be more specific than to tell you there are good reasons to prepare for unnatural threats. Hopefully, the intelligence community and the military will begin to work in tandem with local law enforcement and they will root out the engineers of any plans and put a stop to them. But we can't always believe the government will be successful. As I have said before, think of this like a glorified fire drill where you decide ahead of time a safe place to meet away from danger. That safe place is our new property or Richard's cabin in Aroostook

County, Maine." Jordan said, but then was suddenly interrupted by Lillian.

"Jordan, I don't see any reason why we would ever have to leave our home..."

"Lillian, please," Ed interrupted her. "Just listen and trust that Jordan has a greater understanding of today's reality. We come from a different time and time changes things. What hasn't changed is the fact that we all care for each other. That is why they are doing this, because they care."

"Thanks, Dad," Jordan said, realizing her father was beginning to sense the urgency. "This is 'just in case', remember that. I don't mean to scare anyone, but I need you to have a healthy respect for the unexpected and a genuine fear that there are people out there that continue to plan evil things."

She looked around the room and almost everyone had an expression of quiet resolve. Even Anne had that look of determination in her eyes that meant this family would work towards making a stand if necessary. Lillian was still the only one who didn't get it.

"What, are we all in some kind of Hollywood movie? The biggest threat to America was the USSR and every family prepared for the big one, but the Kremlin ended up falling apart. There are only little gangs of people that hate the West, not a superpower like the Soviets!"

Ed once again tried to talk to her, but she wouldn't listen and stormed off.

"I have made copies of my preparedness journals, the ones I kept during all my training at work. I am not asking you to work on this 24/7. A few times a week, get together and see what else you can accomplish toward a goal of self-sufficiency. I truly hope we will never have to implement any of these plans. If we are attacked, there will be survivors, and I just want our family to be among them," Jordan explained.

That night as Jordan and Leonard lay in bed, curled up after making love, they began to discuss that weekend.

"I don't want to look like a fool, but I really think we are doing the right thing," Jordan said.

"I believe we are too. I want to get the property ready, though. I don't think building a cabin is the first thing we should do," Leonard said.

"No, neither do I. The central issue in survival situations is the availability of resources, not an elegant shelter. Spending money on a big new building isn't the most essential element. Richard and Candace already have a nice cabin, but they are just as unprepared for an emergency as anyone else. We just need something basic, so we can concentrate on supplies and equipment. I have an idea. We can buy a very cheap RV or even an older trailer to set up on our property for basic shelter and spend the rest of our time and money working out the logistics of self sufficiency."

"You are remarkable," Leonard said to Jordan.

"It was your idea, not mine," Jordan said as she laid back down in his arms.

***

Jordan was surprised to see Barrett at work early. As she put her things inside her locker next to her desk, Barrett was having a heated discussion with Agent Johnson. When Johnson left, Barrett yelled in frustration and opened his drawer so he could slam it shut. Jordan didn't say anything. About an hour later, Barrett called Jordan over to his desk and told her that Special Agent Johnson and the higher ranked officials in the agency decided to end Zhao's interviews. They believed Zhao was on target as far as the MSS agents were concerned and for that, he would be placed somewhere in the U.S. and given a new life. However, they did not believe his subsequent Intel at all. They believed the Intel was far-fetched regarding the capabilities of terror groups. Barrett took Jordan upstairs with him to see Special Agent Johnson one more time in hopes of changing his mind. It didn't help. Agent Johnson explained that they had focused their intelligence gathering on all the different factions that Zhao had named. They were all supposed to be part of this huge conspiracy since August 2010 but they had retrieved nothing, not even a mention in chatter. That was the end of the discussion.

Barrett asked Jordan to send the tapes she had made of Zhao's interviews to his assistant for transcribing because he wanted a hard copy of them. For the rest of the week, Barrett was coming in and out of the office frustrated because his request for a review on the matter went nowhere. On Friday afternoon, Barrett asked Jordan and Leonard over to dinner that Sunday evening.

***

They left Lillian's house early on Sunday so they could bring everyone else home before driving to Barrett's home in Sound Beach.

Barrett's wife, a lovely, graceful woman answered the door and welcomed them to their home, which overlooked Long Island Sound. There was a very large deck off the back of the house with a staircase that went down to their dock. When Jordan and Leonard came out onto the deck, Zhao was there talking to Barrett and drinking a beer.

"Jordan, Leonard, thank you for coming. I know I should have had you two over here before now, and I apologize. My wife says I am totally socially inept."

Jordan noticed as they were talking there was a large brand new garage in the side yard with the door open. Inside were pallets of what looked to be bulk food items.

"Sir, what's going on?" Jordan asked.

"Everybody sit down. Leonard, Jordan, a drink?"

"Um, a soda for both of us, sir," Leonard replied.

"The agency has made a final decision about Zhao. They are flying him out on Friday morning to an undisclosed place with a new identity. I know you, and I feel he has more credible information to give us, which is why we're here. We're all going to meet here each night this week, until we know everything Zhao knows," Barrett said, determined.

Zhao began to lay out the details.

"I told you about the structure of their plans. They wanted to begin an attack on December 21, 2012, so they could hitch a ride one of the many doomsday dates. They want to create fear by fulfilling the prophecy, as if there was some cosmic destiny at work. They want to bring the U.S. to its knees and bombing isn't the only way to do that. Weakening your infrastructure and your work force *before* a violent strike can increase its effectiveness.

It will begin with systematic withdrawals of oil deliveries- a problem that can seemingly be solved through negotiations.

As the futile negotiations begin, a biological attack will be initiated to weaken the first responder force. They have been experimenting with several kinds of deadly diseases in space. Zero gravity mutates the germ and increases its virulence by more than seven hundred percent. There would be no stopping it, given that nearly fifty percent of your population now lives in densely populated cities.

Two different delivery systems were designed. Volunteers from each of the factions would purposefully be infected and sent out into the malls, trains, buses, office buildings, military bases, first responder stations, parks and schools. The second delivery system is high tech, and unproven. They have guided systems on 'space junk' that are contaminated with these superbugs that will 'fall' into the United States. They hope that it will spread.

I have also been told they have managed to place a few workers at every oil platform in U.S. waters and at the strategic oil reserves. They don't have to be able to destroy the seven hundred twenty-six million barrels of oil in the reserves, only the mechanism to retrieve them, since they are stored nearly one thousand meters underground. Without oil, the country will grind to a halt. You consume twenty-one million barrels per day, half of which is used by the military. Severely limiting your oil would not only crush your food supply, utilities, and transportation; it would also cripple your response to the threat. Even if you could put together a response with the oil you already had on site, your work force will have been compromised.

One component in these scenarios is what they call 'taking war into the heavens.' Satellites that are armed will strike targets here in the U.S. and would also destroy some of your satellites. It would limit your communications.

Of course, the next strike is the nuclear detonations. I have already told you that they have enough highly enriched uranium for three bombs. These would be ten kiloton nukes that would be ground delivered by an ordinary vehicle driven as close to the target as possible. As you probably know, this size bomb and its delivery method would destroy everything within a three-mile radius of the detonation. Then the radioactive plume would be on the move, leaving a trail of destruction. With only three nukes in their arsenal, they argued over which cities would be targeted. However, since the main goal was to cause as many innocent deaths as possible, cities with the largest populations are at risk. Washington D.C., being the heart of democracy, is their number one target. Their list of cities included New York, Los Angeles, Chicago, Houston, Philadelphia, Boston and Detroit.

The factions of this coalition not directly involved in these attacks will be responsible for additional attacks in more traditional ways. Their plan was still seven days, nineteen missions each day with seven strikes each. Their original plan was to take control of the United States. That is no longer their goal. They thought it more poignant to let you sit and wallow in the contaminated, depleted mess with dreams of what used to be. The additional strikes were at the discretion of the factions responsible for them. I did hear talk of these strikes concentrating on the infrastructure. The San Francisco Bay Area delta was one of them. I can give you as many targets as I can remember this week," Zhao said as he finished with the devastating outline.

Jordan, Leonard and Barrett were overwhelmed with a sense of foreboding. Instead of fear, they were somber. They called it quits for the evening and decided to meet again the following night to hear more details. They wanted to know how they were communicating since the agency couldn't confirm Zhao's information with any digital fingerprints or chatter. Zhao stopped to talk to Jordan as they were leaving.

"I heard you bought vacation property? You will be safe in Maine. I too hope to make it there someday, but I don't know where they are taking me on Friday. Please, take care of your family, Jordan. Family is the most important thing. I will see you tomorrow," Zhao said as he got into an agency car with his security detail.

That night after some much needed alone time, Jordan and Leonard couldn't sleep, so they went downstairs to talk. They agreed the first and most important issue was fine tuning their emergency plans. The second issue was to get someone in the agency to listen to them. That's when it hit Jordan.

"Maybe a different agency will listen," she said.

"They are all essentially from the same bucket of scrabble letters," Leonard joked.

Jordan didn't get it.

"You know, one bucket full of single letters, take three out you end up with FBI or CIA, but they're all from the same... That's not important, what I'm saying is, they are all bureaucrats, bogged down in red tape."

"No, there's one that's different. Who took over when FEMA failed during Katrina? The Coast Guard. Leonard, we already have excellent credibility with them. They will listen and they seem to have the power and integrity to act independently. I'll talk it over with Barrett tomorrow, or better yet, we can wait until tomorrow evening at his house. We can fly up to Boston sometime this week and meet with Commander Godson."

They went to bed looking forward to discussing their idea with Barrett, but at 4:15 a.m. there was a frantic knock at the door, followed by the doorbell ringing over and over. Everybody woke up and Leonard went to answer it. It was Agent Barrett. Leonard opened the door, got him inside and shut the door quickly. Barrett was clearly shaken and Jordan could see in the hall light that he was covered in blood. Jordan turned to the family and told everyone to go back to bed, that it was only a friend of theirs and he was drunk. The family hadn't seen the blood. They brought Barrett into the kitchen.

"Are you hurt?" Jordan said anxiously.

"No, no, it's not my blood... It's Zhao's," Barrett said, distraught.

Jordan put her hand to her mouth. "Barrett, what happened?"

"Chinese agents found him. I'm not sure how yet, but they found him and they hacked him to death with an axe! They're all dead... Zhao... The agents... *They had children*! They must have been attacked right after they got home tonight..." Barrett's voice was shaking in anger. "I got a call from one of the agents on Zhao's security detail, but when I answered, no one was there. I called for back-up and raced over there. How... how could they possibly know it was him? He didn't look anything like himself."

"That's not important." Leonard said seriously. "What *is* important is what Zhao wanted, and that was to prevent this twisted plan, or at least to survive it."

Jordan told Barrett about their idea to approach the Coast Guard Command again. Barrett agreed that it might be their only hope that someone would take this particular threat seriously. Leonard asked Barrett how he left the scene. Barrett told them he spent about an hour sifting though Zhao's belongings and gathering all the notes and hard drives before the agency's CSI team arrived. Leonard went upstairs and got Barrett a change of clothes and an empty messenger bag to put Zhao's effects in. Jordan gave Barrett a towel and led him to the downstairs shower, before putting on some hot chocolate and warming up some bread and soup. A little later they all sat at the kitchen table eating and tried to regain their composure.

"Are we safe?" Leonard asked Barrett.

"Yes, I think so. MSS will not go out of their way to attack U.S. officials. They will only kill U.S. agents if they are between them and their target. They believe it would bring too much attention and possibly stall their plans. The completion of the mission is the number one priority."

They all decided not to wait, but to travel to Boston that day. They packed a bag for themselves and for Barrett since he had never gone home. Then they drove over to the Air Base to catch a HOP to Boston. There wasn't one scheduled, but as a special agent at Homeland Security, Barrett could get pretty much whatever he wanted from any branch of the federal government.

They were in Boston by 11:00 a.m. They took a taxi from the base to the First District Command of the Coast Guard. They didn't have an appointment and were initially turned away from reception, but when prompted to call Commander Godson, he immediately requested they be escorted to his office. They sat down with the Commander for nearly two hours and explained everything. Barrett was the last to speak and there was a minute of silence after he finished. They were all trying to read the expression on his face when he finally spoke.

"This is some colossal shit," the Commander said.

"Exactly our sentiments, sir," Barrett replied.

"I have the power to initiate our own investigation and that is what I am inclined to do. This Agent Johnson sounds like an imbecile. Even if only one of these planned events were actually feasible, it would be too much for the government to ignore. Well, I do find this information credible and I am sorry to say, I do believe these plans are feasible. Barrett and Jordan, you will most definitely be fired by DHS, so resign as soon as you return. I will hire both of you as consultants. I will get you two set up with IDs and cell phones before you leave. SK1, you're fine, you haven't broken protocol, and besides, I'm in charge. I will meet with Vice Admiral Thakur and the Commandant of the Coast Guard to get this investigation going. We will do everything we can to prevent this unholy coalition from fulfilling any doomsday predictions. I'll have my jet take you back to Gabreski."

As they flew home, they all agreed the situation was in the most capable hands possible. That didn't mean it was fully preventable.

"If you think that it's impossible to get uranium into the U.S. just because we are searching for it, think again. All they have to do is hide it in something we already know gets into the U.S. everyday without detection, such as the millions of bales of marijuana. However, if the government can prevent just one of the nuke attacks, they'd be saving thousands of lives." Jordan said soberly.

They arrived back home and Barrett walked to his car and set his things inside. Jordan hugged Barrett.

"Listen, our families are the most important personal issue right now. What we need to do is prepare and pray. There's not much else we can do," Jordan said.

Barrett reached into the car and took an envelope from the messenger bag that contained Zhao's things. He had given only copies to the Commander. It was addressed to Jordan.

"I found this in Zhao's belongings, I didn't open it, and I don't need to know what is in it. We'll talk tomorrow," Barrett said before driving away.

Leonard and Jordan went inside, sat down and opened the envelope. There was a letter, a photo and one hundred thousand dollars cash inside.

73

March 2012

It was a cold crisp Friday morning in Aroostook, Maine and Leonard and Jordan were working on getting the property ready. They tried to travel there during the week so they didn't miss family time at Lillian's on the weekends. Since Jordan was a consultant, she only flew to Boston to meet with Commander Godson twice a month. Leonard had to put in for leave each time he traveled to Aroostook, so he was not able to go as often. The time they spent in Maine was rewarding and peaceful; it was a beautiful place and it was turning into a self-sufficient paradise.

This week they were working on stocking the pond, tilling the ground and installing the windmill. They already had an array of photovoltaic solar panels that provided electricity, but the sun doesn't always shine, so wind power was the back up. They had found several used mobile homes and had them set on permanent foundations that were two stories deep, spread out a little for some privacy. The homes had needed some work, but everyone had worked hard and the homes were now in good shape and fully functional. They had also built a barn and acquired horses, cows, goats, sheep, and assorted fowl. They hired a local teenager to care for the animals while they were away. They had built a rain catchment and storage system and dug a well that provided running water. A septic system for each of the homes would go in next month after the ground thawed, but for now they had an old fashioned outhouse. They had built one concrete building that would serve as a secure storage facility for their emergency food, seeds and medical supplies, along with their tools, guns and additional equipment.

Leonard and Jordan had settled in for the chilly night and were snuggling close.

"Do you think we'll ever have to use this place as a retreat from chaos?" Leonard asked Jordan.

"I don't know. December isn't that far away, but I hope that Commander Godson is successful in preventing this apocalypse. If someone acts to fulfill a prophecy, does that mean the prophecy was true or false? Is it actually a prediction if it is inevitable given our nature? If humans lie, cheat, steal, kill and make war instinctually, is predicting a man-made catastrophe prophetic or simply predictable because it is obvious? Much like predicting the sun will rise tomorrow. If no person on earth tried to make something happen, would that day come anyway? Or, would that day come anyway because it is beyond the bounds of possibility for humans to abstain from their foreordained evil? Why is the voice of the peaceful so much quieter than the voice of the chaotic?" Jordan reflected.

"Wow, you are doing it again. Wheeeeew! Right over my head with the deep thoughts. I'm not making fun of you, I believe the way you think is profound. I just want to avoid thinking of it at all. It's my responsibility to keep my family safe and I don't know if it's even possible to be safe considering we don't know all the details Zhao wanted us to know. He couldn't even keep himself safe," Leonard said.

"Well, he did say family was the most important thing in life. That's what got him killed. I can't believe they were still after him. It had to be payback, because you would have to know he already gave up the major points of the Intel with the amount of time we had him at our disposal. The effort they put into finding him was crazy. They had to have monitored all his mother's mail to finally steal a letter from him. All they knew was that it was from a Post Office box in America. He didn't even use his real name. They got his fingerprints off the letter, let it continue on to his mother and then staked out the U.S. Post Office. I wonder if they bothered to check his fingerprints before they killed him, considering he didn't look like the man they were after. Anyway, he said in his letter to me, he just had to contact his mother. He loved her and wanted her to know he was all right. She knew it was from him, even though he didn't make it obvious in his letter. He gave up his life so he could show the world there are good, righteous people in all cultures who needed to work together to stop the wickedness from taking over."

"We'll be fine," Leonard said confidently. "We're all going to stay up here the whole month of December and not go home until after the New Year."

"You know, I've tried to tell as many people as possible, but everyone dismisses it. Unless it comes from the government as an official warning, people think you're nuts! Commander Godson said they can't issue a warning unless they have specifics, which they can't confirm because they've never heard any chatter. I know they are communicating, they have to be, and I have a feeling I know how, but I can't prove it."

"How?"

"I think they have the time and patience to use the traditional mail, old school, no digital stuff. Instead of personal, hand written envelopes that would bring unwanted attention, they use what everyone ignores: junk mail! I'm going to suggest this to Commander Godson when I go to Boston for our next meeting."

"You may be right, but I'm still hoping that this organization has fallen apart and given up since we know about their plans," Leonard said hopefully.

"Not likely, sweetie."

"I know, I know. I'm just so grateful for Zhao's gift that made this place possible."

***

Friday evening, Leonard and Jordan left Maine and headed for Lillian's house for the weekend. It was slightly warmer in Connecticut than it was in Maine, so Lillian was already planting peas instead of just breaking ground like they were. Leonard drove slightly out of the way so they could stop in Boston and pick up Megan.

That evening felt a little empty. Marshal had completed basic training two weeks prior and was now at Fort Lee, Virginia at school. The school for his particular job as an EOD was unusually long at thirteen months. Because this school was exceptionally long, the Army moved Chloe and Foster to the family housing on base. He wasn't allowed to live with them yet, but he got to stay with them for a few hours if "liberty" was called. Chloe and Foster had driven up to Lillian's to spend this weekend with the family. Foster would be one year old in another month, but was already walking at least six or seven steps before he would fall down. Of course he'd get right back up and go another six or seven steps until he fell down again and he would repeat this for hours until after one of his falls he would just fall asleep on the floor. Chloe told everyone at dinner that as part of his training, Marshal had to jump out of a plane. That bit of news got a range of reactions from gasps to giggles. Jordan tried to keep the sudden sensation of fright in her chest from being seen. Leonard reached under the table and patted Jordan's leg to help reassure her.

Megan and Janice were in a very good mood and were sharing their week's activities with each other and with Carrie. It seemed Megan was doing exceptionally well at school this semester, and if she kept up her present performance, she was looking at a 3.5 GPA. Her best semester before they had to leave school was a 2.9 GPA. Megan said she felt she had a greater appreciation for her education this time.

***

Saturday morning, Roland and the boys were in the garage as usual playing their music. They all had plans that evening to go to another concert of their favorite band, Cyperna, which was back in the area. Anne asked if she could go too, but Lillian forbade her. Anne decided she wasn't going to let her daughter decide what she could or could not do, so she conspired with Thomas to bring her.

That afternoon the girls went to sit on the back porch. The sun was shining brightly and there was a cool breeze. The porch was still enclosed, but several of the windows were open. Everyone was eager to begin discussing the new Suzanne Brockmann book: *Born to Darkness*. Jordan noticed during the entire discussion, Anne had this devilish snicker about her face. Lillian saw it too, but she figured Anne was still mad at her for saying no to the concert.

At dinner that evening Anne was dressed in jeans and a Cyperna T-shirt. Jordan knew something was up. She looked at each of the boys' faces until she saw Thomas trying to avoid her gaze, but he couldn't avoid it for long. Jordan finally locked onto his eyes and he gave Jordan a "what?" expression. Jordan wasn't going to spill the beans, so she smiled at Thomas, relieving him of his anxiety. Lillian would be clueless.

Dinner was over, but everyone was still conversing over dessert and coffee. The kids had left the table and were running around goofing off. Ed and Candace had started the dishes when Ed called to Lillian in the dining room.

"Lillian, do you hear that? It sounds like footsteps."

"Ed, the kids are running all over the place, of course it's footsteps," Lillian answered.

Ed came into the dinning room and asked everyone to be quiet for a minute. Candace grabbed Ashley and held her on her knee as she sat down on a chair. Chloe picked up Foster, placed him on her hip and everyone just looked at each other.

Jordan suddenly said, "Where's Seth?"

As they all looked around they began to hear what Ed had heard: footsteps. The sound was coming from above their heads.

"Thomas run upstairs and get Seth, see what he's into," Jordan said.

Thomas ran upstairs, but yelled, "He's not up here!" as he came running back down.

Jordan got up quickly and ran out the back door and down into the backyard.

"Oh my God! Seth!" she yelled as everyone else came running outside. Seth was on the roof of the house, staring down at the family with that same "What?" expression Thomas had given Jordan earlier. Ed went to the garage to get the ladder and Thomas climbed up and retrieved him.

By 7:00 p.m. everyone had finished putting the dishes away, showered, and had settled in front of the T.V. for a *Harry Potter* evening. Lillian came in frustrated, stood in front of the T.V. and asked if anyone had seen Anne. Only Thomas and Jordan knew she was going, so those left at home just had a dumb look on their face.

Jordan spoke up and said, "Mom, I think she ran away from home to go to the concert."

Lillian gave Jordan a piercing look, stormed off and got her coat as if she was going to go get Anne and bring her home.

Ed walked up to her, took her coat off and hung it up and gave her a big hug.

"She's your mother, not your daughter. I know you're worried, but she wants to live, not sit. This is her choice," Ed explained.

Lillian's arms fell to her side as she gave up. She put her purse away and came into the living room to join the family in watching the movie.

*****

On Monday, Jordan met Barrett at Gabreski Air Base and they flew to Boston to meet with Commander Godson. Jordan discussed her idea about the junk mail with Barrett and he thought it was plausible.

"Credit card offers, phone companies, cruise deals and auto insurance. I get them all, and I throw all of them away. It would be a brilliant way of sending information to all the operatives. No one would give junk mail a second look. I believe it's worth looking into."

They arrived for their meeting and explained the possible scheme to Commander Godson.

"We would have to do a test to see if our suspicions are correct. Since the Chinese and al Qaeda are two of the largest factions in this syndicate, we'll have to pull all the third class mail for two weeks in areas like Los Angeles, San Francisco, New York and Detroit. I'll have to arrange for hundreds of analysts to open them. Let's hope this effort is fruitful. All we've been able to do without more details is to increase security. I don't believe that is enough. We need to interrupt their plans, not just prepare for the fallout or hope to catch them in the act. I will see both of you again in two weeks," Commander Godson said.

The following week Jordan went back to Maine to continue readying their home. Thomas, Seth, and Wesley went with her. Jordan had a detailed agenda about what had to be done, by when, in order for the property to be completed by the end of November 2012. It was slightly warmer then she expected, so she decided to call the septic company to see if the ground was ready for installation. They came out that afternoon and determined the job could be done that week.

The boys added to the wood piles and worked on the outdoor stone kitchen. Jordan had brought some more supplies to put into the storage building. Since there was a credible threat of a nuclear attack and she had been trained to prepare for one, she felt it was prudent to do so, even though Maine would most likely be out of the target areas. One of the items she had been searching for was lead blankets, similar to those that are placed over patients during an x-ray. Jordan was able to collect twenty-five used blankets from various industries and hospitals. She had also bought several of the radioactive protective suits and brought along some sheet lead to line the basements and the storage buildings. Lead doesn't provide protection from every kind of radioactivity, and it does vary on the thickness of the application, but she felt it was worth doing anyways.

On Thursday Jordan was working in the storage building and the boys were again chopping wood. Thomas called for Jordan over the two-way radio and told her Seth was missing. Jordan took one of the ATVs and hurried to where Thomas and Wesley were.

"We were chopping wood and when I turned around he was gone. He was right next to me!" Thomas said frantically.

"Both of you, be very quiet for a minute," Jordan said.

They all stood there not making a sound. Jordan heard some slight movement and a very faint giggle.

"Hear that? He's close. Spread out and look around, but don't call to him, he probably thinks this is funny," Jordan whispered.

They moved out slowly and quietly when a pine cone landed at Jordan's feet. She looked up and searched the canopy and finally saw Seth between the branches. He had climbed almost to the top of a very mature White Spruce.

"SETH!" Jordan cried out, but then quickly covered her mouth.

She decided not to let Seth know, she knew where he was for fear he may do something stupid, like try to jump to another tree, although, Jordan thought, he'd probably make it. She motioned for the boys to come over and pointed to the top of the tree.

Thomas wanted to yell, but Jordan shushed him, "Quietly climb up there and get him, or he may make us chase him."

That evening as they sat around the fireplace Jordan picked up Seth and said, "Mema had a son just like you, you know. I am seriously considering installing a locator beacon somewhere inside of you while you sleep. It will tell me where you are at all times."

"Huh?" Seth answered.

"Never mind."

Thomas went into the bedroom to put Seth to bed.

"Mom, I know you told us we're building this place just in case, but do you know something specific?" Wesley asked, very concerned.

"Yes, sweetie we do have information on a possible serious threat. That doesn't mean it will happen and the government is doing everything it can to prevent it," Jordan said as calmly as she could. "There are threats that are never fulfilled and then there's 9/11 that just happened without a direct threat. Evil will act when it wants to and I am sure it doesn't rest. That is why we should be diligent always, but not so much that we don't live. We could have been overcome with fear, built an underground bunker and moved in there already with ten years worth of beans. I don't call that living. This place is turning into a paradise and its primary purpose is for this family to enjoy it whether for a weekend spot, our retirement or a safe place to come to, if we ever have to. Do you understand?"

"Yes, I get it. I just get scared sometimes from some of the things I see on the news. Why do they hate us?" Wesley asked.

"That's a very complicated question. There are so many different people around the globe that apparently hate us, it would be hard to give a blanket answer. The U.S. isn't perfect, it was an experiment in democracy, but democracy is the only thing going that is reasonably secure and free. In some places it's the survival and ultimate rule of the most ruthless. It's about absolute power, cruelty and greed. The factions that claw their way to the top feel they should be able to treat people within their borders any way they want and an outside nation has no business interfering. Human rights issues, though, are turning into legitimate national security issues for most countries, so the U.N. has started allowing action in response to these atrocities.

Anyway, sweetie, try not to think about it too much. There will always be someone bent on destruction. Even if we achieved peace for a short time, eventually there would be those who took that as an invitation to annihilate those they perceive as weak and take power for themselves. There is no shortage of fanatics with delusions of grandeur and an endless capacity to inflict suffering on their fellow humans," Jordan said with a sigh.

***

It was time once again to go to Boston with Barrett. They flew up to Hanscom AFB and as usual, there was a car sent by Commander Godson to pick them up. Commander Godson greeted them as they entered his office, which was when they saw that Vice Admiral Thakur was also there.

They all sat down and Commander Godson began to talk, but was quickly interrupted by Vice Admiral Thakur, "Jordan, Barrett, your hypothesis was successful."

Commander Godson clarified, "Jordan, Barrett, what the Vice Admiral is saying is that your suggestion about the junk mail was right."

"Yes, indeed, congratulations you two," Vice Admiral Thakur said.

"We intercepted millions of pieces of junk mail in those target areas, and we found something. Within the mountain of assorted ads we found twenty-one that contained letters, instructions and even cash. We have stumbled upon a treasure trove of Intel. Because of you two, we have made some arrests and uncovered details about what I would guess are several of the smaller missions." Commander Godson said proudly as he tried to continue, but was again interrupted by Vice Admiral Thakur.

"AND! The most important news, we have confiscated a WMD!"

"What? You found a nuke?" Jordan said, amazed.

Barrett stood up and addressed Godson and Thakur. "Sirs, thank you. I know this is important to the country, but it is also validation for Jordan and me. No one else wanted to listen to us. The Coast Guard are genuine heroes."

"This one device would have killed thousands of Americans. You two are to be commended," Thakur stated.

"Regardless of what else happens, we can say many lives have been saved. We aren't finished though. We know Zhao's Intel was correct, which means there are supposed to be other nukes out there besides conventional weapons and possibly a biological agent. We don't believe they have figured out how we discovered them. That should yield some more leads," Godson analyzed.

"Sir, what smaller missions did you uncover?" Jordan asked.

"Well, one of them was the California Delta. Several well-placed charges could have collapsed the levees with such force, salt water would have been drawn into the delta contaminating the entire California aqueduct system. If they could react quickly enough, they could close the gates at Bethany Forebay, but that would still leave northern California contaminated and southern California dry. That would mean no drinking water, no water for crops in the central valley- it would have been a mega disaster given how much of the country's food comes from California. This doesn't mean it isn't still a target. The I.E.D.s and money we seized and even the terror cell responsible for this attack can easily be replaced," Godson said seriously.

"The hit on the delta was one of the only smaller missions Zhao was able to tell us about before he was killed. He also told us that any concentration of people or critical services can be targets and those targets could change, depending on accessibility. So, unless you decide to close everything, including buildings, attractions, bridges and roads, it's all at risk," Jordan said, a bit discouraged.

"Well, at least we can officially and publicly announce a thwarted attack on a specific objective. Unfortunately, the President has forbidden us to mention the nuke. The administration feels it would create undue panic. We have made it our mission to tell the public there is always an ongoing threat. Even when we uncover a specified threat and a warning is given, some people still ignore it," Commander Godson said.

Barrett and Jordan went back to New York somewhat relieved that one of the nukes had been confiscated. The fact that it was in the U.S. confirmed their belief that if humans and drugs can be trafficked in without detection, so could a nuclear weapon. They had faith that the Coast Guard would do everything in its power to reveal and stop as many of the attacks as possible. Commander Godson also informed them that the Coast Guard had launched an investigation against Special Agent in Charge Johnson.

April 2012

Lillian's house was as chaotic as the traffic around the 'Arc de Triomphe' in Paris, or at least it felt that way. It was Easter weekend and Jordan met Leonard there after another trip to Maine with Jay, their youngest son and stopping off in Boston to pick up Megan. Jay had that previous week off because of the holiday. That evening everyone took a break and went down to East Haven to their favorite pizzeria for some pies.

"Hey, yeah, we need ten pies, one Sicilian, three with regaut and the rest with extra mutz," Anne told the waiter.

"The Sicilian got the regaut?" asked the waiter.

"Yeah, yeah, and what Foxon Parks you guys want?" Anne called out.

There was a surge of answers all at once.

"Just bring us five each of Birch, Gassosa, Iron Brew, Grape, Orange, Lime, Cola and Root Beer, and bring me some Bud," Anne said as she figured she had it covered.

When they were done the tables were left covered in pizza pie trays with crusts, little paper plates, paper straw covers and a whole mess of little glass bottles with straws sticking out of them.

Saturday morning it was back to cooking, filling Easter baskets, and figuring out if everyone had something to wear to church the next day. Jordan spoke with Janice to see what the status of their emergency closet was.

"We've followed your journals most of the way through. We still have some work to do, but we should be set by December, and like you said, if nothing happens, then we will be super ready for any hurricane, tornado or ice storm," Janice said proudly.

Jordan gave Janice a big hug and told her how much her work meant to her. The boys were back in the garage squealing their guitars and the girls were a few chapters in on the Brockmann book.

That night at dinner Ed asked Jordan if she had any news. Jordan hadn't told the family any details. Time was ticking closer and closer to the date Zhao had named, and Ed, as the patriarch, wanted to know what he was really up against.

"Dad, I don't like giving everyone nightmares, but I guess you should know. The Coast Guard confiscated one of the nukes," Jordan said, knowing this would forever change their outlook.

"One... of the nukes?" Ed stammered as the family gasped. "What exactly do you mean by 'one'?"

"Their plans are to deploy seven."

"SEVEN, are you kidding me?! SEVEN!!" Roland yelled.

"WHAT? WHAT?! Oh my God!" Carrie cried.

Jordan tried to speak calmly over the confusion. "People, this is why I needed you to get prepared. Commander Godson and the Coast Guard are doing everything they can to unveil and shut down these attempts, but realistically, with a tidal wave of various attacks, each implemented by just a handful of people, it is like looking for the proverbial needle in the haystack."

"There will be more than just nukes?" Janice asked.

"Unfortunately, yes. Unless we can stop it," Jordan said.

There was an awful quietness about the table, so Jordan was glad she had waited until everyone had finished eating.

That night, snuggling in bed, Leonard and Jordan wondered if they did the right thing in telling the family the major details.

"When some people hear such devastating news, they withdraw from living their life. I don't want that for anybody. Maybe I should have just let them be totally oblivious to the threats. If nothing happened, they would be none the wiser," Jordan said.

"That's not what your father wanted. He wanted the truth and he wanted them to hear it," Leonard said firmly.

"I know, I just feel so guilty. It's the time spent in fear anticipating tragedy that is truly debilitating. You can't change a thing about the coming situation by worrying or torturing yourself about the what ifs. There's plenty of time afterwards for that... That is, if you survive." Jordan said, realizing she started sounding like those nuts building the bunkers, and thinking maybe they weren't so nuts after all. "Leonard, do you know that you are my God-given solace? When we're alone, snuggling and talking, it's comforting- almost like the rest of the world doesn't exist."

"I love you too, even though you didn't eat your green beans and drink your milk when you were growing up," Leonard said.

Jordan smiled as he held her tightly and they fell asleep.

***

All day Sunday there wasn't any music coming from the garage. Jordan still felt guilty about telling them of the serious threat. Only the children were still playing as usual, oblivious to what their parents now knew. Richard and Candace came onto the back porch, which was now fully open again, and approached Jordan, who was sitting in the rocking chair with Ashley sound asleep on her lap.

"Ma," Richard said, "if things even slightly go sideways, I'm going to pack my girls up and head to Maine. I won't even hesitate."

"I am so glad to hear that, Richard. You are a rock and I couldn't ask for a better son-in-law. Have you guys started stocking your cabin?" Jordan asked.

"Not yet, but I will get on that this week," Richard promised.

"Ma, have you talked to Marshal or Chloe?" Candace asked.

"No, since he has been in school he hasn't answered his cell. Chloe is visiting her mom in Oregon for a while. Of course their dog is still here. I think I'll call and talk to her and her mother. I know December is still several months away, but it's unsettling when we're separated from parts of the family. We all need to keep doing what we're doing and if that time ever comes- like you said, Richard, if it goes sideways- then we're outta here," Jordan said, trying to lighten the mood.

Ashley woke up and started squirming. "Ashley, what's a matter, do you have ants in your pants?" Jordan asked as she tickled Ashley.

"Nope, I don't have ants in my pants and I don't have anything in my head either," Ashley blurted out as she jumped off Jordan's lap and ran away. They laughed.

That afternoon at dinner Jordan stood up to talk.

"I am so sorry I ruined everyone's Easter. That was not my intention. If we let this fear of someone, something, somewhere at sometime rob us of even one happy moment together, then it's like it has already happened. I mean, that's what we fear, right? An end to our normal everyday life, our routines of work and play and most importantly the give and take, the interactions between us that make us part of humanity. So, I came to terms with it this way. I prepare because it's necessary, but I do so in a disciplined manner. Then I intentionally, purposefully dismiss it as exaggerated nonsense, as if the critics were right. I pretend as best I can to believe today and tomorrow will be the same old same old. Imagining a devastated world is so easy today given our advanced graphics in movies, so we have to force ourselves to imagine what is around us intact. Our neighbor mowing his lawn, the McDonald's up the street still serving billions of burgers, paying bills and the sun still rising and setting. I would rather be blown away right in the middle of a dinner with all of you, than to anguish over impending doom and miss a moment of family time."

Dinner was uncomfortably quiet.

Leonard and Jordan packed up the car to head home after not talking to anyone after dinner. As they were getting into the car, Ed came out and gave Jordan a big hug.

"Give everyone time to process this, Jordan. I mean, this is life-changing stuff and it's got to work its way around inside their heads, but eventually they will come to grips with it and settle into a new reality. It's almost like grieving."

May 2012

Barrett and Jordan were discussing the threat of an oil blockade with Commander Godson.

"Jordan and I have come to the conclusion that this is possible, sir. Major segments of our daily life depend on petroleum product deliveries several times a day. We're talking about food production, transportation, power... It would be a devastating domino effect. Within one to three days this country would come to a standstill. Stores would be empty, gas stations closed, massive amounts of crops would be unharvestable or would be sitting in some depot, rotting. We've analyzed the logistics of our oil deliveries. Of the fifteen countries we acquire most of our imported oil from, eleven have controlling factions that are a part of this conspiracy, another three would be easily intimidated and the only hold out would be Canada. Unfortunately, Canada has every terrorist group in the world operating and training within its borders. I don't like those odds," Barrett said grimly.

"We depend on these countries to sell us the oil," Commander Godson replied. "There isn't much we can do if they say no, so all we can do is prepare for the aftermath. We have been disseminating general emergency preparedness information through every possible avenue, trying to get people to stock six months of food, water and other supplies in their homes. I don't know how many people have complied. Just the reports on our failing infrastructure should scare you enough to stock up. Unfortunately, hoarding gasoline doesn't work- it breaks down after a while, so you would have to rotate the reserves constantly. I am going to authorize at least some gasoline storage for the

Coast Guard to keep operating in case the U.S. strategic oil reserves are inaccessible."

***

Mother's Day weekend at Lillian's the atmosphere seemed to warm up a bit. Ever since Jordan had informed the family about the threat, it had been rather icy during the visits. On Saturday afternoon a single faint guitar was heard coming from the garage. Everyone lifted their heads from their books, T.V. and video games to listen. It was Jay- just a few notes, a few measures, then an entire song. Within an hour the boys had joined him and music was once again filling the house. Ed and the guys congregated near the pond and were talking about the best fish to stock. By evening the girls had gathered on the back porch and taken out the book they had started in March. Janice was in the den playing with the kids and they could hear her singing some pop tunes. As the evening started to sound like old times again, Anne was disturbed by a pounding noise that seemed to come from the den.

"Hey, 'Beyonce,' what the heck is going on in there?" Anne called out to Janice.

Janice stopped singing long enough to answer back, "Nothing, Seth is just playing with his construction set."

The singing started again and so did the pounding. Jordan decided to go check it out. It was, after all, Seth. Jordan came around the corner into the den and saw Janice performing in front of the mirror with her back to Seth, who was standing in front of the wall near the door. As Jordan turned toward the wall, she exclaimed, "Oh, for God's sake!"

Janice spun around and everyone else came running into the den. Seth was standing in front of a wall that now had seventeen softball-sized holes in it. The whole family collectively dropped their jaws on the floor. Seth had unscrewed one of the legs from his trampoline (bought to help work out his energy) and used it as a battering ram on the wall.

"Honestly," Lillian said with a sigh, "it looks like Swiss cheese."

"Yes, yes it does," Wesley said as others nodded their heads in agreement.

Everyone started to look at each other and that's when Anne started giggling. The laughter spread like a wave and before long, people were laughing so hard they were in tears. When Roland tried to talk, the words were labored with deep honking sounds in between.

"O… O… Only a Marshal, Wh ... where does ... he ... come up with this stuff!" As the laughter calmed, Thomas picked up Seth.

"You know buddy, you are going to have to get a job to pay for that," Thomas teased.

"Okay Daddy, I go to work!" Seth said proudly.

Later, Leonard and Jordan were sitting in bed that night amazed at how the evening ended.

"It feels right again," Jordan said.

"Like your dad told us, they just needed time," Leonard said relieved.

"Now, *I* need some time. Come here, short one," Leonard said flirtatiously as he grabbed Jordan and they fell back onto the bed.

Mother's Day dinner that Sunday was a big affair. They had roasted leg of lamb and all the fixings. During dinner they got phone calls from Marshal, who of course heard all about Seth's antics, and Chloe, who was still staying with her mother in Oregon. Anne stood up and first thanked everyone for such a beautiful Mother's Day. Then she addressed the family.

"Ed, we were all shocked when Jordan gave us the news and some of us were mad at you for asking her to tell us. We just had to adjust. You were right, there will always be some sort of threat simply because we exist. Often I see something on the television about a doomsday. I guess all kinds of cultures have had prophecies about a Judgment Day. I think the stories were trying to keep people moral. Who knows, maybe the good Lord will come and take us all home before this happens. So, just like waiting for the rapture, we need to just live instead of wasting one precious day."

June 2012

The sun was shining brightly on the water, so much so that it was blinding as the boys tried to fish at Lillian's. Thomas, Wesley, and Jay were down at the pond lounging in the Adirondack chairs, feet up, sunglasses on and their poles between their crossed legs. Seth was the only one moving. He was throwing rocks into the pond, so there was very little chance of the boys catching anything. Megan was home from school with her newly earned B.A. in mathematics with a minor in music. Jay had also graduated with his B.A. in nursing. They had had a congratulatory dinner for them the previous night and showered them with gift envelopes. Megan had stood up and thanked everyone for their generosity, since she knew how long it must have taken for each family member to have saved up that much money. In total she received forty-five hundred dollars to spend any way she wanted.

"I know you want me to do something great with this money, so Janice, it's yours, go back to school," Megan said decidedly.

Roland just smiled, Carrie started crying, Janice was over the moon with excitement, Ed put his arm around Lillian and slapped his knee and Anne said loudly, "That's family, that's what I'm talking about!"

Everyone else cheered.

"Well, sweetie, you're going back in September, you don't have to wait until January now," Carrie said, still crying.

It was a night to remember.

The boys came back from the pond embroiled in a debate about the NBA finals with Seth following behind them covered in mud. Wesley took him toward the garden to hose him down. The girls ran out of the garden about five minutes into Seth's hosing when Wesley turned the hose on them. The rest of the boys ran back down the hill to get some of the action. It was a free for all.

The boys were going to a Cyperna concert again and this time Anne didn't have to sneak out of the house in order to go. After dinner, Anne was the first one ready, sitting in the living room waiting for the boys, dressed in her new jeans with red flaming embroidery down one leg and her Cyperna T-shirt.

"This time I want to stand closer to the mosh pit," Anne said determinedly to Thomas.

"Okay GG," Thomas replied.

"Can you throw me in, so they can pass me around like a beach ball, Thomas?" Anne asked.

"I don't think that would be a good idea, GG," Thomas answered.

***

On Monday morning Jordan and Barrett flew to Boston for their meeting with the Commander.

"I think we should discuss the germ warfare component this time, sir," Jordan said.

"Yes, we should get to that today, but right now I need to update you on our efforts," Commander Godson replied. "Let's see, we've expanded the junk mail inspection to fifteen regions and we've uncovered fifty-three new pieces of terrorist communications. We returned these pieces of mail back into the mix and followed them to their destinations. Among the captured are a Sikh extremist cell from India with a vial of an unknown substance, a Yemeni cell with ties to al Qaeda which had I.E.D.s to target LAX, an Iraqi individual with surveillance tapes of the National Mall, and an Iranian cell where every member worked at the Perdido Spar oil platform in the Gulf of Mexico. We also got a Mexican drug cartel member with assassination plans targeting President Abdullah Gul of Turkey and assorted others from FARC, members of Australian-Somali based al-Shabaab, a cell of Sri Lankan Tamil Tigers, Chechen guerillas, members of the Islamic Movement of Uzbekistan… Oh, yes, this is new, an American Neo-Nazi chapter and a militia group with plans to destroy Temple Emanu-El in Miami and Touro Synagogue in Newport. I think if you needed a definition for 'bandwagon,' this would be it. We have not, however, located any of the other nukes.

Back to what you wanted to touch on today, Jordan, the vial we found with the Sikh cell. We don't know what it is yet, but we're thinking it may be harmless- just a trial run. I am speculating that several of the operations will need trial runs leading up to December."

"This unholy alliance is vast and it has set its sights on destroying the democratic ideology," Jordan said.

"Many of these groups have been oppressing people in their own countries for decades. It's all about getting more- more money, more power and more eternal glory, but they will propagandize that it is a fight in defense of their religion," Barrett said.

"Unlike the countries that want a commodity such as oil available on the free and open market, creating energy security to benefit all, China wants to privatize the sale of oil and other necessary resources by making direct, lateral deals, trading outside the global marketplace, such as their three billion dollar back door deal with Iraq in 2008. We know from Zhao that China's ultimate goal is economic and resource hegemony and the elimination of their only competitor: the United States. That's precisely why they have been allowing the U.S. to become indebted to them, so we could collapse. They have spent the last decade or so traveling the globe with the riches they have obtained by trafficking and by manufacturing almost every single thing we buy. They have been paying off unscrupulous political regimes to control the natural resources of the world. They own the oil, the gas, the refineries, power plants, copper, cobalt, manganese, uranium, water, wheat, corn... The list goes on. The world is for sale and China is buying. They will use this unholy alliance to further their agenda and then they will crush all of them without hesitation," said Commander Godson. "We have to do everything possible to keep democracy alive. This threat of Communist world domination is more virile than ever before, even during the cold war."

"We all used to laugh at the villains in cartoons that had delusions of grandeur about taking over the world. I guess globalization has made it feasible," Jordan said.

"We have discussed the fifteen countries that we obtain our imported oil from before, right here in this office. These back door deals for oil that we have uncovered are extensive. China has negotiated these 'out of marketplace' transactions with not only Iraq, but also Saudi Arabia, Kuwait, Ecuador, Brazil, Colombia, Venezuela, Mexico, Nigeria, Angola, Algeria, Chad, Cameroon and Russia," Commander Godson explained.

"That's all of them except Canada," Barrett exclaimed.

"Yes, we know. All they have to do is say stop and the world stops delivering oil to the U.S. and the dominoes start falling. We are doing our best, convincing the public and the government that we have to operate without imported oil. That is the challenge we have to meet in the next few months, along with protecting our own oil production," Commander Godson answered. "We have our work cut out for us."

July 2012

Ashley and Seth were running in circles in Lillian's back yard with sparklers and mini American flags in hand. They had all just come back from the fireworks display at the town beach. It had been a really busy Sunday that had started out with the boys playing their latest piece in the garage, the girls finally finishing Brockmann's *Born to Darkness* and everyone else fishing. They celebrated Independence Day that Sunday (even though the Fourth wasn't until Wednesday) with a traditional afternoon BBQ with hamburgers, hotdogs and all the fixings. It was already way past bedtime, but the kids were all still excited about the day's activities. It was nearly 1:00 a.m. by the time everyone settled down and went to bed.

Leonard had that week off, so Monday morning they all packed up and headed off to Maine along with Richard and Candace. They planned to work on a secondary storage building with a two-story basement that they believed would be more secure than the original one. It would also serve as an underground shelter if they needed it.

"I think I qualify as one of those nuts that build underground bunkers now," Jordan said ironically.

"I think we have to remember that during the Cold War when there was a realistic threat of nuclear war, average people built bomb shelters in their backyards. Some people still build panic rooms right in their homes," Leonard said matter-of-factly.

"You're so sweet," Jordan said as she embraced Leonard and kissed him. "I don't know what I would do without you."

"You'd be lost!"

They walked out to the new storage building where Wesley and Jay were stocking the shelves with the supplies they had brought with them. As they approached, they could hear the boys having a heated debate over the last few MLB games. As with all their debates, it went on for hours in fits and starts.

That evening, as they all sat around the fire in the courtyard of the outdoor kitchen, enjoying the sweet smell of BBQ baby back ribs cooking over the fire, they remarked about how quiet it was. Occasionally you could hear a fish or toad splash in the pond, a wolf call or the dogs barking at some smell that came across their noses.

"I can't believe how many stars are in the sky. I don't remember it being so crowded up there," Wesley said with amazement.

"That's because we live near a populated area with too much light pollution," Jay explained.

"I wonder how Marshal is doing at A.I.T.? I spoke to Chloe a few days ago and she was expecting a call from him this weekend. She said he's supposed to get a break sometime in October. I hope so... I miss them all so very much," Jordan said.

"Isn't Chloe coming back soon?" Leonard asked.

"That's what she said. I wish they were home already. We could at least spend time with her and Foster, but I guess she needs time with her mom before they start the military nomadic lifestyle," Jordan said wryly.

"When we get back home, I'll find out if Marshal can have visitors yet and we'll take a ride down to Virginia to see him, okay? I miss him too," Leonard said.

The following day Richard got up at 4:00 a.m. and took Wesley on his boat down St. John's River to fish.

They got back around 8:00 p.m. with a cooler full of trout. Leonard and Jay spent the day working on their horse-drawn carriage.

Jordan had been up early too, but had spent hours talking to Barrett and Commander Godson. It seemed that suddenly there were zero junk mail intercepts.

"I think they caught on," Barrett said.

"I agree," Jordan commented, "but I don't think they're going to make it easy to catch them talking on cell phones, knowing we can intercept their conversations. My guess would be digital junk email written in code, which they may have been using all along with the traditional stuff."

"Well, we may have a few more leads this week. We've arrested Special Agent Johnson. It seems he purchased a villa, in his sister's name, on St. Thomas, for eight hundred thousand dollars. Why do these people think they're going to live happily ever after? Anyway, he'll be interrogated here by C.G.I.S. this week. You're both welcome to come," Commander Godson said.

"No thank you, sir. I am with my family up at our home in Maine and we won't be back until next week," Jordan said.

Barrett said he was just too busy and really didn't want to see the traitor.

***

Leonard and Jordan packed up the boys on Friday and followed Richard back down to Lillian's house. By the time they arrived, Roland and Thomas were already in the garage playing. Anne was sitting at the drums banging away, keeping them warm for Wesley. Ed came inside from the backyard where he was firing up the grill for dinner and asked Jordan about Agent Johnson.

"What the hell was he thinking? If there is anything on this earth that really bugs the shit out of me, it's law enforcement who betray everything they are supposed to uphold!" Ed said angrily.

Leonard patted Ed on the back to try to calm him down as he walked with him to the back porch.

"Have you heard from Marshal yet?" Lillian called from the living room. Jordan turned the corner and went into the living room where the girls were.

"No, Mom, I haven't heard from him directly. I did talk to Chloe this morning. She got a five minute phone call from him earlier and he said he was doing fine. He is expected to get a few days off during October. Chloe said she plans to go back to the base in September. Leonard discovered that he's allowed visitors on the weekends, so we're going to take a drive down there at the end of the month. I can't wait to see him," Jordan said excitedly.

Later, Leonard and Jordan were snuggling in bed.

"Do you think if there's some cosmic doomsday, that it won't make a bit of difference what we try to do to prevent it?" Leonard asked.

"I truly believe we have a choice. If this flock of vindictive, selfish butchers just cast away their contempt for human life and decided to join those from every culture trying to achieve peace, we may have a chance. I have the distinct feeling that through their blinding hatred in trying to destroy us, they will destroy themselves and cause pain and hardship for their own innocent people," Jordan said with a heavy heart.

"What about a natural disaster?" Leonard asked.

"Well, you plan the best that you can. Nature doesn't have evil motives, it just is what it is. Humans, on the other hand, have motives. I think I will reserve my fear for an enemy that thinks and yet still executes," Jordan said thoughtfully.

***

On Monday morning Jordan flew up to Boston with Barrett for another consult with Commander Godson. When they arrived in his office, Vice Admiral Thakur and two other men were also there.

"Barrett, Jordan, nice to see you again. Please sit down," Admiral Thakur said. "As you know, in the past six months we have tried to coordinate with as many law enforcement agencies as possible to look for the slightest indication of the commencement of hostilities on our own soil. As you pointed out, Jordan, in one of your research papers, our northern border has been an unabated source of criminal facilitation for some time now. To assist in our efforts to secure that seemingly endless, unmanned wilderness, we have sought and achieved an alliance with our tribal government counterparts. In the First District, we have consulted with the Iroquois or more appropriately, 'The People of the Six Nations.' If you know your history, you'll know they were an inspiration for our democracy. We have a good working relationship with them- in spite of our ancestors, which says a lot for the character of the Six Nations. So, I'd like to introduce you to the Haudenosaunee Nation's representatives, Nathan Fougnier and Dale Fadden."

"A pleasure to meet you," Jordan said.

"Greetings," Barrett said.

"I have already briefed our guests on everything we know about the threats to our nations. We need to do what ever we can do, collectively, to protect and preserve our homeland," Godson said.

"I understand you have studied Native American Nations, Jordan," Fadden said.

"Yes, sir, I concentrated on North American native peoples in cultural anthropology," Jordan answered.

"We are also coordinating with local LEOs and tribal governments from all the northeastern states because of what we discovered this past week. The Forest Service and the St. Regis Mohawk Tribal Police, which is part of the Six Nations, apprehended a group of Somalis that had come across the border from Canada near Hogansburg, New York with a Mexican drug cartel guide. They were carrying AK-47s, several IEDs and a map leading them to the Boston Medical Center," said Godson seriously.

"Do you know when they were supposed to carry out this attack?" Jordan asked.

"No indication at all. For all we know they were heading for a safe location until December or they could have been heading directly to Boston. We have not been able to get anything out of them, yet. We believe they were supposed to stay at the casino and wait to be picked up," said Fadden.

"Do you have any idea why they would choose that hospital?" Barrett asked.

"I think I do," Jordan interrupted. "First, it's a soft target- more psychological damage, and second, if the big cities are hit, level one trauma centers safely outside those cities are where survivors would be sent."

"We must also anticipate that they will target first responders and CBIRF. That's the Chemical, Biological Incident Response Force," Barrett added.

"Good point, Barrett," Godson said. "I have some other disturbing news. Three countries- Cameroon, Chad and Nigeria- have withdrawn their oil from the global marketplace. I speculate that they are testing the waters, but it looks like China put them up to this. We will have to make up the shortfall from our other suppliers. The mistake with oil dependence was made decades ago. If it had been up to me, we would have eliminated that dependence then. This is going to bite us in the ass and render us ineffective if they expand this embargo. I will increase the Coast Guard's reserves of gasoline, oil and lubricants as a precaution. We will have to rotate the stock as we discussed before, but I will not be grounded when our country needs us the most!"

That evening, Jordan and Barrett invited Fadden and Fougnier to dinner. They wanted to get to know them better before they all left Boston. The men were very aware of the serious consequences to both the U.S. and their tribal nations if these threats were acted upon.

"Our nations have a symbiotic relationship and despite the early history, I believe today's Americans and Native Americans desire the same future for their children; peace, democracy and freedom. I speculate also that given the power to change things, many people across the globe also want the same for their children," Fadden said.

"Barrett and I feel the same way. There are grassroots forces at work in every culture trying to stem the tide of depravity, but unfortunately greed, power, lust, religious fervor and hatred are more popular than peace and brotherhood," Jordan replied.

"Civilization means to work together for the common good. Most of these groups are looking out for themselves and their personal agendas," Fougnier added.

They all exchanged their contact information and were pleased they had made new friends.

***

Leonard and Jordan were getting ready to go to Lillian's for the weekend. Leonard was given liberty at noon on Friday, so they were getting an earlier start than usual. Thomas, Wesley and Jay had gone to the basketball courts to pick up a few games, so Leonard and Jordan were watching Seth. Leonard and Jordan were in their bedroom packing their bags for the weekend when they heard the key turn in their bedroom lock. Their house had been built in the early twentieth century and most rooms had doors with skeleton key locks that locked from the outside. Jordan walked over to the door and discovered it was locked. She knocked on the door to see if she could get Seth's attention, but all she could hear was laughter coming from downstairs. Leonard started to yell for Seth, but there was no response.

"Well, this is great, we've managed to get ourselves locked in our own room," Leonard said, exasperated.

"We can hear him, why can't he hear us?" Jordan asked.

They continued to knock on the door and call out to Seth without any reply from him.

"Wait, I hear something… That's the front door! Someone is knocking on the front door!" Jordan said.

Leonard and Jordan listened while Seth answered the door by himself.

"I hear a voice… It isn't the boys… Oh man, it's Patterson from the housing office," Leonard moaned. "Patterson! Hey, Patterson!"

"Leonard, is that you? Where are you?" Patterson called.

"Come upstairs, Patterson!"

Patterson sheepishly walked upstairs. When he got to the upstairs hallway, he could hear Leonard on the other side of the bedroom door.

"Patterson, we're locked in. I think my grandson has the key," Leonard said.

Patterson could be heard through the door laughing his ass off.

"Patterson, do you think you could stop laughing for a moment to go get the key from Seth?" Leonard said, annoyed.

Leonard and Jordan could still hear the stuttering cackles as Patterson went downstairs to the living room where Seth was playing with about six skeleton keys. Patterson took all of them back upstairs to the master bedroom and tried them one by one until he finally set Leonard and Jordan free. Leonard grabbed the keys from Patterson and tried to give him a serious look, but Jordan started to giggle which made it impossible for Leonard to keep his composure. The boys had a good laugh too when they returned three hours later.

They invited Barrett and his wife to Lillian's house for Sunday dinner. After dinner, Leonard, Jordan and Barrett had a short but important discussion out by the pond.

"I received a phone call from Godson on the drive out here," Barrett began. "Jordan, he will probably call you too. It seems that when Chad, Cameroon and Nigeria withdrew their oil from the global marketplace, we turned to Algeria to make up the difference. Now, Algeria and Angola have withdrawn their oil from the market. We are assuming, but we don't have confirmation yet, that China is pulling the strings there too. We never should have turned to another African nation to take up the slack. We should have gone to

Canada. I said so to Godson, but we'll see whether the administration will listen to a Coast Guard Commander.

This past week was very irritating waiting in line for gas. Several stations closed. On top of that, the grocery stores were out of many items. They announced to the public it was just a temporary delay due to a small logistical issue. They figured that would suffice for a while. This isn't going to get better. I think they are going to whittle away at our suppliers, causing the administration to chase its tail while they work out new deals, and diverting our attention from the eight hundred pound elephant in the room."

"An eight hundred pound elephant is a yearling," Jordan said with a laugh. "A grown elephant can be fifteen thousand pounds. Although an eight hundred pound anything in a room would still be very impressive."

They all laughed.

"We should laugh. Number one, we need it, but number two, the administration is going to screw this up. They don't get it, still. I think the Coast Guard is the only agency that gets the gravity of the situation," Barrett said.

"I think you may be right," Leonard said ruefully.

***

Jordan's cell phone rang, rang and rang until she finally answered it. It was 3:00 a.m. on July 18, 2012. Jordan looked at the caller I.D. and saw it was Godson.

"Commander Godson, what's up?" Jordan inquired as she put him on speaker.

"Jordan, at midnight we were informed by every supplier except Canada that they were withdrawing their oil from the market. Within a day, we should see some serious repercussions. This is more than not being able to fill gas tanks. Our average food items travel nearly fifteen hundred miles to get to our plate. Food won't be harvested from the field if the enormous combines and tractors can't operate. If you can't harvest the food, grocery shelves will be empty and animals won't get fed. If you can't feed the animals, there is no meat, eggs or dairy products. Oil and gas are the very core of our economy- they power our cars, trains, planes, farm equipment, factories and critical services. People, products and services will be grounded. A massive chain reaction is about to start. If people haven't planned, desperation will set in very quickly. During Katrina it only took three days before the veneer of civilization came off and people were rioting," Godson said soberly. "I'm hoping the government will freeze prices to stem the chaos."

"What should I do, sir?"

"Just stay by the phone, Jordan. If you talk to Barrett first, let him know. We have to analyze this move and try to discern what course and pace they may be planning."

"The question I have is, why would they give us time to regroup if they are still planning on more than an economic cluster fuck?" Leonard asked.

"That is something we need to analyze. I believe this is a litmus test for vulnerabilities. Rough estimate is we produce half of our oil and we import the other half. The U.S. military alone uses half that oil. So, if the U.S. military operates normally, that means one-fourth the normal amount of oil for everyone else, because that is all we get from Canada. If we shift oil from the military for the needs of everyone else, we will be more vulnerable at home than we already are by having most of our troops overseas," Godson speculated.

"Instead of observing and waiting, they could decide to proceed with the terrorist acts during this chaos. Barring those additional acts, it will still take us about eighteen months to make the adjustments needed to operate the rest of the country. I am talking about substituting the missing oil with alternatives. Even then, there really aren't adequate substitutes for oil," Jordan added.

Leonard called his parents and Jordan called Ed to tell them what was going on and assure them that the best course of action right now was to stay at home. Then they tried each of the other family members in turn, with no success until Jordan reached Richard.

"I think I will take the girls to Maine now," Richard said. "I am not taking a chance that this is the beginning of it all. I can come right back and go to work if the plant is even open, but the girls can stay there."

"That's a relief- at least I won't have to worry about *them*," Jordan said with a sigh. "Text me and keep me updated as to where you are. You have the mobile station, right?"

"Yes, CB in one car, mobile station in the other and ham radio at the cabin," Richard said.

Leonard went to work at the station and, as he expected, it was hectic. All the crews were out doing shoreline patrols. The station had sent a van to the housing area first thing to pick everyone up so they wouldn't have to use their own gas to get to work. Reports were coming in by late afternoon of more gas station closures and frantic buying at grocery and department stores. By 10:00 p.m. the local grocery stores were apparently empty.

Richard had left for Maine around 8:00 a.m. with both vehicles and several cans of gasoline. It was an eleven-hour trip and Jordan was worried about them.

Richard finally called around midnight and said they had arrived safely. They did however have a problem in Lawrence, Massachusetts at a rest stop. Richard had walked Candace and Ashley to the women's restroom and when they returned a group of young men was trying to break into the back of his truck where the gas cans were. Richard ran after them with a big stick and they took off. He said they damaged the window to his camper top, but had not gotten in. Richard told Jordan he was going to come back the following day.

***

Jordan's phone started ringing again a little after 7:00 a.m. on July 19, and this time it was Barrett.

"Barrett," Jordan said as she answered her phone, "Did Godson finally get a hold of you?"

"Just got off the phone with him. There is an outbreak of some currently unknown respiratory disease in Miami- at this point it looks like a new strain of the 'flu. Godson is going to get some more detailed information, but what we know right now is that the incubation period is quick and so far there are forty-two people in Mount Sinai Medical Center in Miami."

"Well, the question is, why the oil situation now? We expected trial runs with outbreaks, even serious ones leading up to the main event, but we expected the oil embargo right before it," Jordan said.

"There may not be a reason why now, other than they changed their minds to throw us off. Maybe they want us to think the main event is coming now, so we go and expend some of our resources, or maybe they have changed the time line all together."

"We need to look for any additional signs that it may be materializing now instead of December," Jordan said seriously.

"Agreed. Talk to you soon. Be safe."

"And you."

Jordan was anxious for Thomas and Seth to get home. She had tried calling Thomas again after Barrett called, but he didn't answer. Jordan fielded several more calls from Barrett and Godson. Four additional cities were reporting severe outbreaks: Las Vegas, San Francisco, Kansas City and Cleveland. Godson had received confirmation that it was a new strain of the 'flu, but was still awaiting news on its specific characteristics.

That morning several of the Coast Guardsmen that worked the housing office came by to ask for volunteers to go with them to the local farm. They had made arrangements that in exchange for labor, they would receive a bushel of food for each worker. It was only four miles away so all the guys decided to ride their bikes. Only one person had to drive an electric cart over there to carry back the baskets. The grocery stores were already empty and there were not going to be any deliveries any time soon. Because of Godson's directives, the Coast Guard had back-up plans for most contingencies. Their plan was to give the food to each military family that needed it. Jordan's house didn't need the food, but they believed it was their duty to help.

Leonard and the other Guardsmen that worked out at the station had been picked up by the station's van. Leonard called home around 9:00 a.m. and told Jordan how crazy it was at the station. They were getting calls from the local community to see if they had emergency food, water and even batteries, even after they spent months providing outreach programs centered on emergency preparedness. They were also getting calls for assistance from waterfront residents whose boats were being siphoned of gasoline.

Godson called again.

"Jordan, I have Barrett on the line also. I am afraid it is bad news. There are now twenty major cities reporting outbreaks and the CDC has declared it to be a pandemic. One of those cities is Bridgeport, Connecticut. The CDC also has told the administration that its virulence is beyond anything they have ever encountered. In Miami, where the first reports came in, there are now fifteen thousand known cases, two hundred dead and they have had to close the hospitals. There is little chance a vaccine can be developed in time, because it is already past the point of being contained. This didn't spread from Miami, it independently started in these other cities. Our in-country assets are reporting catastrophic losses from this pandemic in Juarez, Mexico; South Australia; Pyongyang, North Korea; and Sichuan Province in China. It seems that the creators of the virus didn't take adequate precautions. I think we know what comes next," Godson said gravely.

"Shit, this sucks. Why now?" Barrett said.

"They simply did not want to wait until December," Jordan suggested.

"It's time to go," Godson told them.

"I guess we can expect the rest of the plans, whichever ones they are capable of, to come about at some point," Barrett said angrily.

"Keep in touch. I will try to give you updates as often as possible," Godson said as he signed off.

"Jordan, you need to get out of there, now," Barrett urged.

"When I can get everyone organized, then I will be on the road," Jordan promised.

As soon as Jordan sent the "time to leave" text to everyone, she began taking the emergency supplies out of the basement and bringing them up to the living room. Wesley and Jay arrived home, but they hadn't read the text she had sent them.

"What's up, Mom?" Wesley said as they saw her emerge from the basement with another box full of rations.

"It's time, we have to go, now! Get your GOOD bags and anything else you are responsible for and if Thomas, Seth and your father don't get back by the time you are done, start on theirs," Jordan said determinedly.

The station van arrived with Leonard and all the other Coast Guardsmen to help their families get on the road. Leonard ran inside and the first thing he did was hug Jordan and the boys.

"Did you hear from Thomas?" Leonard asked worriedly.

"No, where could he be?" Jordan wondered.

The boys put the carrier on top of the car, then went back to grab essentials from the house.

"Leonard, we have a problem. We can't take route 95 through Connecticut, because one of the diverging contagions was launched in Bridgeport. We could take the Orient Point Ferry to New London if it's operating- we have to check- otherwise we have to drive up to Queens and then go north another way."

"I'll call the Coast Guard station up at Orient Point instead of the ferry office. They are probably overwhelmed at this point," Leonard said.

He contacted the Chief at the Orient Point Station, but the news wasn't good, the ferry had run out of fuel early that morning.

"Jordan, there's not going to be any ferry to Connecticut," Leonard yelled from the basement.

Leonard and the boys were nearly finished packing the car, so Jordan tried to call Thomas again, and he finally answered.

"Thomas, where are you? We need to go, now!" Jordan said hurriedly.

"I will have to meet you up there, Mom. I'm sorry, I should have been home, but Diane and I spent the whole night talking. When I got your messages about the outbreak I thought this could be it. I can't leave her here- she's Seth's mother. I am trying to persuade her to come with me. I love you, but I'll get there when I get there," Thomas said as he hung up the phone.

"Thomas! Thomas!" Jordan tried to call him back, but he didn't answer.

"Leonard, Thomas isn't coming, he's with Diane," Jordan cried.

"He'll be fine, he knows what he has to do and he knows he's responsible for Seth. He will leave in time to get him out of there, I know it," Leonard said firmly.

Jordan calmed down enough to ask where the boys had gone and Leonard told her they had gone into the garage. They walked to the car and saw the boys in the garage.

"Boys, it's time to get the dogs into the car," Leonard instructed.

Several minutes later the boys came around the side of the house with Kaila and Thor.

"Man, this is going to be crowded without Thomas's car," Jordan exclaimed.

As they packed the animals inside, they could see tightly-packed cars leaving the housing area and fellow Coast Guardsmen walking toward the gate.

"What's going on, Leonard?" Jordan questioned hesitantly. Then she looked into Leonard's eyes and knew he wasn't coming with them.

"No!" she cried. "No, no, *please* no, we have to stay together!"

"You and the boys have got to get on the road," Leonard said sadly as he tried to comfort Jordan. "I'm sorry, I want to be with you, but we're part of our country's defense and I have a duty to the Coast Guard."

Jordan just cried as Leonard held her.

"Wesley, Jay, you are going to have to keep each other and your mother safe, especially since Thomas and I won't be with you. I will be there, I promise, as soon as I can. I will be there," Leonard lovingly told them.

As they piled into the car and Leonard tightened Jordan's seat belt, which had a child attachment on it due to her height, the boys pointed a remote into the garage starting the stereo. They had set the CD player on repeat and it was blasting loudly across the now empty military housing neighborhood.

Wesley turned to Leonard and Jordan and said quietly, "We felt we had to say something."

"Appropriate," Leonard said simply.

"You're right. If the enemy arrives, they might not get the message, but at least they'll be irritated," Jordan added grimly.

As the car pulled out, the pounding lyrics of "We're Not Gonna Take It" were clearly audible.

No, we ain't gonna take it...

There ain't no way we'll lose it
This is our life this is our song

We'll fight the powers that be just
Don't pick our destiny cause
You don't know us, you don't belong...

We don't want nothin', not a thing from you...

We're right, we're free
We'll fight, you'll see...

Jordan cried as she drove away looking into the rearview mirror. She could see Leonard standing in the middle of the road, waving goodbye as the other Coast Guardsmen walked towards him.

Meanwhile, Ed and Roland were packing their vehicles while everyone else, even Anne, was bringing all the supplies to the front porch.

"Mom, you need to sit down, the girls and I got this," Lillian said.

"I have to help, it keeps my mind off of everything," Anne said with a catch in her voice. "We are coming back, right? Eventually?"

"We don't know, Ma, we don't know what's ahead at all, we just know we have to go."

Megan, Janice and Carrie were practically running with the supplies to try to keep Lillian and Anne from carrying as much.

"Get as much of the fresh produce out of the garden as you can and put it in one of the coolers, girls, okay?" Ed suggested as he was tightening down the carrier.

"Ed, Roland, we got a text from Jordan. There is an outbreak in Bridgeport, so she said to follow the infectious disease protocol in her journal," Carrie called out to the guys.

"Do you know where the journal is?" Roland asked.

"I do- it's in the medical bag," Megan said.

"Roland, keep your gun nearby in the car, loaded. I'm sure there are going to be people who are willing to get what they need any way they can and we have family to protect. As the situation becomes more serious, the roads may not be safe," Ed told him quietly.

The girls clicked the button on their remote to their stereo in the garage, playing the same defiant message Wesley and Jay had. They finally got on the road at noon. Ed decided to drive past Diane's house so he could see if Thomas was still there. If he was, Ed planned to take Seth with them, but when they arrived, only Diane's parents were there. They told Ed that Thomas had left about forty minutes earlier.

Ed headed to Interstate 95 and estimated that the trip should take them eleven hours with no traffic. There were no reports of the pandemic north or east of Bridgeport yet, but the contagion was moving rapidly. When they entered the highway, they knew immediately this was going to be one hell of a pilgrimage. The highway was backed up as far as you could see, bumper to bumper of vehicles full of people, cars starting to pile up alongside the highway, abandoned after running out of gas, and the people from those cars walking or hitchhiking.

"Damn it, I shouldn't have come this way," Ed bellowed.

Ed got on the radio and called to Roland, "Hey, stay close to my car- we can't get separated. I'm going to find a different route."

"Hey, Pop, have everyone put on a mask and don't open your windows," Janice told Ed over the radio.

It took them three hours to get to New London where Ed decided to turn off Route 95 and head up Route 395. It wasn't much better, but Ed was glad they made the switch. Jordan had texted them to let them know the outbreak in Boston was spreading rapidly and Route 395 was a good fifty miles west of that.

Jordan and the boys had peeked at Highway 27 and decided not to get on- it was jammed packed with travelers, abandoned cars and people. They guessed that Route 495, being the only other major highway on Long Island, would also be a mess, so they took a secondary highway. Jordan hadn't wanted to head towards New York City, considering it was expected to be a target. Ed had texted her after stopping at Diane's house to let her know Thomas had left.

Richard was apparently heading north again after picking up additional items at his house, but exactly where he was, Jordan didn't know. Jordan kept their radio tuned to the local P.E.P. (primary entry points) station to hear constant emergency broadcast updates. When they reached Rocky Point there was a message detailing the massive congestion in Port Jefferson from people fleeing Bridgeport via ferry possibly carrying the virus. Jordan decided to get off that route and continue on back roads. It was slow going, and by 1:00 p.m. they had only reached Douglaston, in Queens. Since Jordan's car was still moving, people would walk alongside and knock on the windows, wanting to get in.

Jordan was just about six miles from the Throgs Neck Bridge, but she needed to get back on the highway to cross it and get off the island. As they finally crawled off the other side of the bridge, Jordan stared out the window toward Long Island Sound with the sailboats, some leaving and some still moored. Every time they had traveled to Lillian's this way she would gaze at this peaceful, beautiful sight. Suddenly, there was a flash of light coming from behind them, as bright as a million suns. Jordan could only see a small glimpse with her peripheral vision, but knew exactly what it was.

"Boys, a nuke!" Jordan yelled frantically. They knew what this warning meant. "Don't look, cover your ears, but keep your mouth open!"

Jordan could see the people outside the car and in the cars next to her looking back towards New York City. Within a few seconds the distinct deafening boom of a nuclear explosion blasted across the boroughs. Jordan watched the people outside her vehicle hold their eyes and cry in pain.

"Do not take off your masks! Wesley, open the medical bag and take out the IOSAT! Jay, open up the tool kit and take out the radiation suits and the blankets! We have twenty minutes to get underground before the plume is on the move!"

People were on the ground running as cars were trying to push through the traffic. The P.E.P. station was blasting sirens and warnings that a nuclear bomb had been detonated near the Empire State Building. Jordan headed for the exit, which was only fifty feet away, maneuvering through the chaos. Everyone who hadn't been blinded by the flash was trying to get on the highway in an attempt to outrun the plume. She looked for an underground parking structure and drove to the very bottom floor, three floors underground.

"Quick- lay several of those radiation blankets over the car, then get back in," Jordan told the boys as she tossed Wesley a blanket.

Meanwhile, Leonard and the other Coast Guardsmen saw the mushroom cloud from the station. Leonard's heart sank as he tried desperately to call Jordan. Communications had already been spotty in the past week due to power shortages, and now it was anyone's guess what link in the communications chain had been broken. The men were ordered to suit up and take the two Response Boats-Medium (RB-Ms) down to The Narrows where CBIRF was setting up Radiation, Triage, Transport and Treatment System (R.T.R.) stations. R.T.R.1 sites were in Zone3 in Manhattan. Zone1 was the designated "no go" zone and Zone2 was the heavy damage zone, while Zone3 was the moderate damage zone. On Staten Island, an R.T.R.2 site was set up on the edge of the dangerous fallout or light damage zone, outside the perimeters set by the fire departments, for any survivors that might make it out of Manhattan, Kings or Queens County.

"The plume is headed this way in an ESE direction. We need to travel around it to get to Staten Island," said GM1 Harris.

Thomas had decided to take Route 91 north, which would bring him through Hartford. He had been getting Jordan's text messages, but didn't reply or call because he wanted to concentrate on just getting there. They had left around 11:30 a.m. and, like everyone else, had run into congestion. Thomas had the radio tuned into the P.E.P. station as they announced that every major city was reporting the 'flu, which was spreading even to isolated communities. They were in Hartford when the emergency broadcast came on about the nuclear attack on New York City. Thomas quickly tried to call Jordan, but there was no service. He feared the worst and started to cry.

"I should have answered the last time she called! I could have told her that I loved her," Thomas said, not knowing if he would ever get the chance to do so again.

"Mema's okay," Seth told Thomas.

Thomas felt there was no choice but to continue through Hartford. The highway was the most direct route. If danger arose, he was prepared to do whatever he had to do to protect his family.

Richard was further along than everyone else. He had taken a secondary highway through Connecticut and Massachusetts in between the major cities. He had made it to Winchendon Springs, on the border of New Hampshire, by the time Jordan was getting to the Throgs Neck Bridge. Many of the towns up there were far apart and had only one or two roads in or out. When he reached Munsonville there was a barricade of trucks across the road and men with guns. Richard got out of his truck, but didn't approach the men. He stood close to his door and told the men he was just passing through on his way to Maine, that he didn't want to stop.

"Nope. Nobody in, nobody out. We have to protect our own. You may have the virus or want to take our supplies," one man explained.

Richard didn't tell them he had all the supplies he needed, not knowing if they would try to take them from him. He just turned around and went back toward Keene. Richard figured he would have to take one of the interstates, so he went west of Keene and took Route 91 north along the border. He came upon a few more closed towns and had to backtrack, but finally crossed over into Maine near Wilson's Mills. He tried to contact Candace with the mobile station, but was still out of range.

Marshal's class had only been at school for four months, but the country needed them. Their division was deployed as foot soldiers around the perimeter of D.C. checking individual vehicles for all things suspicious. The recruits were not allowed cell phones, so there was no way to contact Jordan, Leonard or Chloe to let them know where he was. About an hour after the explosion in New York City, Marshal was stationed with a platoon at the entrance to Benning Bridge northeast of the city. Their platoon leader noticed that a man was behaving nervously after being asked to get out of his vehicle. He had started to reach for something, but the soldiers pulled him out of the car before he could grab it. After securing the man and the vehicle, it was discovered the car was packed with explosives with a detonator in the glove box. After interrogation, the man revealed his mission was to destroy the Benning Bridge to prevent people from leaving the city.

***

Later, it was determined that the nuclear explosion in New York City had been carried out by an al Qaeda cell that had been based in New York and had worked illegally at a nursing home for two years. It was a ten-kiloton, gun-type, Improvised Nuclear Device (IND) constructed from highly enriched uranium, purchased from a former nuclear weapons plant worker in Russia. It was detonated by hand, in the back of a van that was driving past the Empire State Building. This device had a destructive and EMP radius of about three miles. The plume of radioactive material that started to move after the mushroom cloud reached its maximum height of fourteen thousand feet had a width of twenty miles. That area was designated the dangerous fallout zone and was being mapped by the Interagency Modeling Atmospheric and Assessment Center. It would begin to claim more victims as it moved with the wind. In a city of more than eight million people, the death toll would climb to several hundred thousand within a few days and continue to kill over time.

The administration initiated Operation SCATANA-Security Control of Air Traffic and Air Navigation

Aids- which grounded all flights and activated the Nuclear Emergency Response Team (N.E.S.T.) to search for a second nuclear device. Through Operation Fly NEST, these seven-man teams were given priority over the air space to hunt for additional nukes.

Within an hour of the first strike, the timing devices on several IEDs set in place by the Juarez cartel were triggered. A series of strikes, just as Zhao had described, were initiated around the perimeter of the nuclear blast zone in New York, Connecticut and New Jersey. Several key bridges, McGuire Air Force Base, Naval Submarine Base New London, Yale University, hospitals, cell towers, and critical utilities were hit. They were set to go off one at a time, making it seem like the barrage would never end.

In Detroit, despairing television viewers witnessed something that at least momentarily brought hope to their failing hearts. A local mosque called the F.B.I. at the P.V. McNamara Federal Building and asked for their assistance. When the agents arrived they handed over four men belonging to an al Qaeda cell and a van containing another IND.

The men had clearly been interrogated. The spokesman for the community, Jamal Mohammed, came forward and spoke to F.B.I. Special Agent in Charge, Matthew Reed. "We've uncovered this al Qaeda cell and their weapon in our community. Their intended target was Detroit, and they were supposed to deliver and detonate this scourge today. This country is our home. It is our children's home and they love and play with your children. This would be like murdering someone who has eaten at our table. We choose to live in peace with our neighbors, and choose only to wage jihad against the intolerance in our own hearts. We hope you will do the same."

Within a few days nearly half the city would be dead from the virus, but they died united. This one momentous act of goodwill and bravery kept the city from total chaos as the virus spread.

***

The roads had become very dangerous, so Ed and Roland kept pushing to get as far north as possible before they had to get out of their vehicles. They passed through Worcester, Massachusetts where their cars were accosted several times. The guys pointed their guns at the assailants and they backed off. They headed east again through Lowell and finally stopped near Lawrence so they could fill their tanks. They pulled into a rest stop that looked empty and after scouting out the area from inside the car, Ed and Roland got out, unlocked the cargo carriers and retrieved the gas cans. They were filling the tanks when three men came out of nowhere with knives and demanded the keys to the vehicles. Just then, Anne came around the back of Ed's van with the 9mm Beretta and pointed it at the men.

"Put those fucking knives on the fucking ground, now!"

The men started to laugh.

"What the hell are you gonna do, you old bat?" one of them said.

Anne fired at the man and hit the knife right out of his hand, taking off two of his fingers. "Does that answer your question?" Anne yelled.

The men ran off, leaving their knives on the ground. Ed took the gun from Anne and gave her a big hug.

"Are you okay, Ma?"

"Of course I am," she said and they all got back in the car and headed out.

Leonard and the other Coasties left for Staten Island, heading for the U.S. Coast Guard Station New York, just north of what remained of the Verrazano-Narrows Bridge, careful to travel around the edge of the fallout zone. When they approached the station, they expected to see multiple crews of National Guard, Army, Marine CBIRF and the Disaster Rapid Response Medical Force fully operating. What they found instead was just a handful of responders at the R.T.R2 site.

"Where is everyone?" Leonard asked one of the Marine CBIRF soldiers.

"It was the virus, sir. It spread so rapidly it decimated our troops and civilian first responders. All the bridges and tunnels into Manhattan have been destroyed. Even if we could set up an R.T.R.1 site inside Manhattan and transport victims to this site by boat, there is nowhere to forward the victims to. The Collection Centers are already filled to capacity because there are no open hospitals, and even before they were hit they were inundated with pandemic victims. We have to treat whomever makes it out of the city with what we have here," the Marine said.

"These sites are set up for triage only! You can't treat severe burns or perform surgery," Leonard said.

"We know. There will be multitudes of black toe tags, dead or dying, and they will pile up quickly because we also have nowhere to bring the corpses," the Marine said, overwhelmed with the situation. "Our response is supposed to work like a well-oiled machine, but every component in that machine has been corrupted. We are on our own."

"We'll patrol the Narrows and the Hudson for any survivors trying to swim off Manhattan," Leonard told the Marine as they turned around to head back to their boat.

Suddenly there were sirens coming from the P.E.P. station again. The emergency broadcaster announced there had been another nuclear explosion, this time in the heart of America's democracy and leadership: Washington D.C. The detonation site was near the front of the Capitol building. Everything within a mile was vaporized, everything within two miles was in ruins, and everything within three miles was damaged, but standing. No one knew who in the line of succession to the presidency was still alive. The nuke had exploded two hours after the one in New York. The barrage of secondary attacks began only fifteen minutes after detonation, against the same type of targets- military bases, bridges and tunnels, hospitals, universities and critical utilities. People had started to evacuate on their own after the attack in New York, but they didn't get far. The roads had been gridlocked since the virus started to spread.

Richard had finally gotten within one hundred miles of the cabin.

"Candace, you there?" Richard tried the Mobile station again. "Candace?"

"Yes, I'm here, we're okay. Where are you?" Candace questioned anxiously. "Richard? Richard?"

There was no answer.

"Damn, I am really sick to my stomach with all this! When will this day end?" Candace sobbed.

Richard didn't know what to say to her even if he could keep the connection open. He knew she was getting enough horrifying news from the radio. When he had traveled through the smaller towns north of Bangor he had seen some gruesome sights. There were hundreds of bodies, some neatly wrapped and some haphazardly piled along the road. The further north he traveled, the fewer bodies he saw. He couldn't help feeling both lucky and guilty for having been prepared.

***

The smaller factions of the alliance were carrying out their individually designed attacks across the country. The Mexican drug cartel had hit the border regions hard, trying to eliminate their opposition in the drug trade, but hatred can be blinding. The virus they seeded along the border was not only eliminating the law enforcement infrastructure that was trying to end their reign of violence, but also killing their customers, their runners, their families and wiping out entire towns on both sides of the border.

Near Las Vegas, several objects had been seen falling from the sky, which drew the curious to the crash sites. They carried the debris with them back to the city. These items were the guided, contaminated space junk China was experimenting with. Las Vegas was overcome with the virus within hours.

***

After the close encounter in Lawrence, Ed headed for Route 95 again near the border of New Hampshire. He was hoping the chaos and mess had thinned out this far north. Except for filling the gas tank, they really didn't have to exit the vehicle at all, thanks to Jordan. They had a portable toilet, stored water, food and an emergency radio. All they needed was a clear road. They had been listening to the reports of the devastation in New York and D.C. and everyone wondered about Jordan and the boys, but nobody said anything. The pandemic was spreading so quickly it was impossible to outrun- all you could do was protect yourself. There was too much to think about; so much, it was hard to think at all.

They had driven about twenty miles from Lawrence when the P.E.P. station started its sirens again. It was more dire news; a third nuclear weapon had been detonated in Los Angeles, two hours after the blast in Washington. Lillian and Anne started to cry. Ed called on the CB to Roland to ask if he heard the news. Carrie, Roland and the girls felt like life had just stopped. They were all overcome with mournful feelings for so much loss, it was debilitating. They wanted to pull over, get out of the car and just break down, but they couldn't. They had to keep going.

There were only a handful of cars trying to maneuver down the highway through the abandoned ones, some with drivers still at the wheel, obviously deceased. Very few of the hordes of foot travelers were moving any more. They guessed these were people who had fled Boston, carrying the virus with them. Ed decided the threat of contagion was too dangerous and again got off the highway. He took a shot in the dark and tried to reach other family members on the mobile station, with no response.

Thomas, alternating between highway and back roads, was getting frustrated and angry. He just wanted to get his family to safety. Diane and Seth had asked a few times to stop, but he refused, telling them over and over how dangerous it would be to stop. They eventually stopped asking, but he felt like he had failed them somehow.

After a little while, he tried to calmly talk to them. He told them he would try to find a place they could pull over to pee, but that would be it. Every time he heard news about additional attacks, he just cried. He cried and yelled in anger at the world, the people on the side of the road, the other cars, the pandemic, anything he could scream about. He drove aggressively through the obstacles all the while holding his gun in his hand.

He was on the back roads going around Springfield because he figured the virus would cause an exodus out of the city. He finally made it northeast of the city and drove a little out of his way to a recreation area near Quabbin Reservoir. No one would be vacationing right now, so maybe it would be empty. He drove around the vast camping areas and the long lonely roads from one private cabin to another. Thomas saw one or two people near the entrance, so he drove around to the more remote area between the two sides of the lake, and again drove around looking for any movement. He chose a cabin that had a particularly long private driveway that could be watched from inside. He broke into the house and made sure no one was there, then called for Diane and Seth to come inside. Thomas barricaded the door, then sat down on the couch, broke down and cried uncontrollably.

"I'm lost without my family," he moaned.

"We're here, Thomas," Diane said quietly.

"What? You don't even want to be here with me. Admit it!"

"You're right, Thomas. I didn't want to be with you. I wanted more from life. I was selfish, I'll admit that. Hell, I wanted more than just to be loved and it took the end of the world to slap me hard enough to wake me up to see what I had. You know, I remember your mother always saying something about wanting to be the person that knows what she has, before it's gone. Smart lady, I should have just listened, but noooo, I had to find out the hard way..."

Thomas interrupted her speech, grabbed her and Seth and just held on for dear life.

***

The North Koreans and Russian Mob forces were in charge of the West Coast strikes, and after the nuclear blast in L.A., the secondary blasts began detonating across the region. Operatives traveled north to the San Francisco Bay to the delta and detonated the bombs they had planted there two days earlier, collapsing the levees. Unlike the previous cell that got caught, they were successful. The collapse was so violent it drew in the salt water from the northern San Francisco Bay, contaminating the delta all the way down to the Bethany Forebay Reservoir. No one was there to close the gates, so the contamination traveled all the way to southern California.

Ironically, most of the factions within the alliance that carried out missions on the ground were dead from the virus. The alliance had promised each faction that their own agendas, whatever those goals were, would be handed to them by the expected new world super power: China. What they didn't foresee was that unlike China and al Qaeda, whose roles were highly technical and carried out primarily from a distance, their group's involvement expended relatively high numbers of boots on the ground and put them in proximity to the infected areas. China and al Qaeda figured this arrangement had the potential to wipe out most of the alliance, especially the ones they considered morally or socially inferior. China secretly also felt that way about al Qaeda, but for now they were a necessary evil, too well organized with a global presence the other groups did not have. They could deal with them later, after the rest of the competition was gone.

Most of the major bases had been hit from inside either by secondary explosive attacks, or by wiping out a portion of their personnel with the pandemic. The

Department of Defense had the training, money and even the fuel to implement rescue operations, but unfortunately the soldiers themselves were incapacitated by the virus. The remainder of the U.S. forces that were not infected were spread out across the world in Afghanistan, Libya, Africa and South East Asia. When the virus started to spread across the world, the military quarantined all these soldiers.

For years, these bases had unwittingly welcomed operatives right through the front gate. Almost all the work crews engaged to perform labor (contractors like road crews and construction) had illegals working for them with forged identifications. Most of them were honest people glad to have a job, but there were enemy operatives among them, hiding in plain sight. What the opposition didn't count on was the relatively small force of the United States Coast Guard.

***

Leonard, the other Coasties, and the handful of Marines were still on Staten Island attempting to make the masses of survivors comfortable. Every hour they scooped up more victims from the waters. As they pulled alongside the station dock with more survivors, they could see something coming towards them from the Lower Bay. The Coasties, Marines and the few other first responders turned around and looked toward the bay. Within minutes, the 378's-United States Coast Guard High Endurance Cutters-came into view. The dolphin HELOs and the OTHBs (Over the Horizon Boats) disembarked from the cutters and hurried toward the station. Godson had arranged for two Navy Hospital Ships months earlier to be stationed thirty minutes southeast of the city, out in the Atlantic. The HELOs would transport victims classified as immediate according to the triage system. The other patients deemed minor would be transported by boat to the Coast Guard Cutter, which would in turn deliver them to the hospital ship. Godson had the same scenario operating outside D.C., Los Angeles and a half dozen other locations.

Hundreds of members of the relatively small factions represented in the alliance such as Venezuela, Colombia, Georgia, Russia, and Somalia had visions of taking over some cities by combat force, staking claim to their newly conquered territories before the bigger players got theirs. Fortunately, they seriously underestimated the resolve of even sick and injured Americans, especially Texans. The factions had sheltered near Waco until after the nukes had detonated, fully expecting to run rampant over Dallas, San Antonio, Austin, Houston, and Amarillo. As soon as they entered these cities, every Texan that could lift the barrel of a gun put them down where they stood, never even having fired a shot.

***

Richard finally got within twenty miles of the cabin and called Candace again on the mobile station.

"Richard, thank God, are you all right? Where are you? Have you heard from anyone else?" Candace asked anxiously.

"I'm all right. I'm about a half hour away. I haven't heard from anyone else, but I'm going to go over to Leonard's place first to see if anyone is there."

Richard went over to Leonard's place to look around. He used their ham radio to call over to the cabin and told Candace no one was there. She cried and cried until she felt like her heart was tearing open. Richard went home to Candace, and when he pulled into the yard, Candace and Ashley came running out into his arms. He spent the night calling over the radio, trying to contact anyone in the family.

***

The following day the U.S. was in a state of collapse. Three major cities were devastated, and subsequent attacks on infrastructure made it almost impossible to mount any type of ground response locally or militarily. The virus had already claimed a little more than one hundred million lives. Another one hundred million were in different stages of severe sickness, injury, or suffering from radiation poison and would probably die within the next week or two. The remaining one hundred million were displaced, alone, without adequate communication, food or water and in great danger from roaming gangs fighting over the last vestiges of the American dream that would give them power in a new reality where the rule of law and civilized behavior were matters of opinion.

***

Ed and Roland were still traveling north having to change routes and even directions depending on what they encountered. Just like Richard, on smaller routes they came across towns that were barricaded. When they reached the Maine border, their vehicles were attacked by a large gang that broke one of their windows. They took off quickly, firing their weapons over the mob, but when they finally were able to slow down, Roland realized he had a flat tire. They all got out and surrounded their vehicles with guns in hand, even Anne, until Roland was finished changing the tire. After dodging a multitude of obstacles, they finally made it to Leonard's. When they piled out of the vehicles, Carrie collapsed on the ground and the tears began to flow. Megan and Janice ran to comfort her.

"Roland, get into Leonard's place and try the radio, see if you can get in touch with Richard and Candace," Ed instructed. "Everyone else go inside and try to calm down."

"Ed, I got in touch with Richard. He's okay. Candace and Ashley are with him at the cabin," Roland said. "They're on their way over."

"If you and I had this much trouble getting up here, I can't imagine what Jordan will have to endure, if she even made it out of New York," Richard said to the guys moments after he arrived at Leonard's.

"Thomas left before we did, so we should have heard something from him. We need to keep our hopes up," Ed said.

"Leonard and Marshal are in the midst of that mess fighting. Who knows where they are?" Carrie added tearfully. "I am so truly thankful that you guys have made it here. I feared that we would be alone, that our entire family would be just the three of us, but I want all of my family back."

"Okay, right now we need to unload the vehicles and start doing normal, everyday things. We'll take turns at the radio, trying to reach them. No news isn't necessarily bad news, considering the state of the communications," Ed said firmly.

The second night after these terrible events, sleep still eluded them. On the third day, approximately at sunrise, Janice was at the radio, calling out to the family one by one. Suddenly she got a response. She yelled to wake up everybody in the house.

"It's Thomas, it's Thomas! He answered me!"

"Hello, hey are you still there?" Thomas called out over the crackling airwaves.

"Yes, yes! Thomas, this is Janice. Where are you?" she said anxiously as the rest of the family hurried into the room.

"I am about an hour away on, I think it's Route 11 north. You won't believe what we've been through in the last three days. Is everyone all right?"

Ed took over the handset. "Thomas, this is Ed. Who's with you?"

"Diane and Seth," Thomas answered.

"Have you heard from your mother or your brothers?"

"They're not with you at the house?" Thomas asked desperately.

"No son, I'm sorry. Richard, Candace and Ashley are here, as is Lillian, G.G., Roland, Carrie and the girls. We haven't heard a word from any one else."

***

"Boys, wake up," Jordan said softly.

"Are we still okay, Mom?" Jay asked.

Jordan turned on the flashlight to read the dosimeter.

"Yes, Jay, we're still okay. It's been three days. I think we should try to get out of here. We need to keep our suits on until we know where the radiation traveled. We need to stay sharp. By now, we shouldn't expect normal civilized behavior from anyone we encounter. We have to travel fast and try to avoid being noticed."

For the past three days, Jordan and the boys had stayed underground in their covered van. The only time they opened the sliding door, on the side facing the wall, was to let the dogs out to do their business, and to toss out their toilet liners. They had everything they needed inside the van. Jordan would check the dosimeter every hour, even though if the radiation was getting to unsafe levels it would sound an alarm. The worse part was they were very sweaty in the suits, but being annoyed by a little discomfort was the least of their worries. Not knowing the fate of the family was weighing heavy on their hearts. They talked about it often and tried to keep positive.

They started the van and drove up the ramp until they saw daylight. It was a beautiful sight, but sad considering the losses. They were emerging into a changed world. Jordan turned on the emergency radio and listened to the recap of the last three days' horrors and the current conditions of the roads, that they were pure anarchy and considered extremely dangerous. For the first two hours, it was slow, trying to drive though the remains of people and cars. It was eerily quiet except for the noise the tires were making running over the debris. They didn't see a single living person until they got past Stamford, Connecticut. As they got closer to Bridgeport they could see chaos on the streets below them. They hoped no one would see the single vehicle crawling along the interstate just above them.

"Mom, they saw us!" Wesley yelled.

Jordan and Jay looked down onto the roads below them as one by one, people took notice and started up the embankments. Jordan had been trying to drive as gently as she could over the debris, but now she had to step on it. She sped up, but a few members of the crowd caught up to the van. They pummeled the van with rocks, baseball bats and crowbars. The dogs lunged at the windows as the mob got close. Jordan managed to break away from them a few times, but they would catch up again when they faced denser debris. Two men climbed on top of the van and began to unscrew the cargo carrier. Jordan hit an open patch of road and sped up again and one of the men fell off the van. She jerked the steering wheel to try to dislodge the second man-he, too, fell to the road, but so did the cargo carrier.

"Mom, get off the interstate! Take Route 8 over to the Merritt Parkway," Wesley suggested frantically.

"We need to get away from the cities," Jordan said as she approached the parkway and determined it was too much of a mess.

They got onto a secondary road heading northwest and worked their way over to Route 7, which was more of a scenic route, but when they got close to Danbury they ran into another riotous mob. Not only were they beating the van, men started to reach into the van through a broken window and one of them grabbed Jay's arm. The dogs lunged at the man while Jordan grabbed her handgun and threatened the rest of them. Just then, a blast from a shotgun hit the front of the van. The shot had come from a man just ahead of them. He pointed the gun directly at Jordan, ready to shoot, but Jay leaned out of the broken window on the passenger side and shot the man in the shoulder. Jay shot into the air two more times as Jordan took off through the scattering crowd. This road was relatively clear of debris, but had scattered mobs. They kept their speed up for a few more miles with the boys defensively positioned out their windows.

"We can't keep this up. The roads are too dangerous and the car is starting to overheat. We need to travel on foot to somewhere these mobs won't go," Jordan told the boys.

Jordan drove to Bull's Bridge, a historic covered bridge in Kent that was surrounded by waterfalls, woods, hiking trails and most importantly, next to an entrance to the Appalachian trail.

"How are we going to know which way to go?" Jay asked.

"Guys, the Appalachian Hiking Trail starts at Springer Mountain in Georgia and goes all the way to Mount Katahdin in Maine. We just have to go north-it's the best choice we have," Jordan told them.

Jordan and the boys stripped the car of everything they had left and resources they might need from the van itself such as the rubber mats, a little cushioning, and piping from around the seats. They already had the most important stuff, their GOOD bags, medical bag and tool bag. The problem they faced was trying to bring as much water as possible.

"We're going to have to build a travois," Jordan told them.

"What's that?" Jay asked.

"Native Americans used to build sleds out of available materials that their dogs and horses could pull. They used them to transport a variety of things. We may need to build two, but Kaila and Thor are both capable of pulling one."

That night, Jordan and the boys took off their radiation suits and set off on the Appalachian Trail toward their family refuge. The Trail meant they probably wouldn't have to deal with terror acts or mobs anymore, but they would be on their own in the wilderness and the occasional small town. Jordan estimated it would take them two months to reach their destination in Maine if they had to walk the entire way. They brought their portable ham radio with a solar charger, but left the large mobile station with the van. Every hour Jordan sent out a message in case they were in range of another radio operator that could forward a message further along. Ham operators were a trustworthy bunch.

The water they laboriously carried would only last for part of the trip, after which time they would have to rely on their other skills and tools to obtain safe drinking water from lakes and rivers. They slept outside, made fires, occasionally hunted, and foraged for wild foods when available, saving their rations for areas that may not be so fruitful. Sometimes they were able to stay at the trail cabins as long as they were empty. They did run into a few other hikers, but they passed each other cautiously without making eye contact.

One night they came close to a trail cabin, but it was occupied, so they waited awhile to see if the occupants would leave. One of the hikers was injured, so Jordan decided to take a chance and see if they needed help. It was a family of four and the young boy, maybe thirteen, looked like he had fallen. They seemed to have some standard camping gear, but were not equipped for a long trek in the wilderness. Jordan and the boys approached carefully with their hands close to their weapons. The family wasn't armed. They greeted each other and Jordan told them she could help. The boy had broken his radius and had several lacerations that needed stitches, which Jordan took care of. Jordan and the boys took off afterwards and went back into the woods.

They had been hiking for about twenty days when they arrived at Mount Tabor in Vermont. According to the trail map, they had traveled about one hundred eighty miles.

"I think we should stay here a couple of days and rest. We'll find a cabin, get comfortable, reinforce the travois, refill the water jugs, and possibly give someone a chance to answer our radio messages," Jordan said.

After two days Jordan and the boys got back on the trail heading north. They had traveled about three hours when they heard someone heading toward them, so they moved cautiously. Horses came into view and when they got close, Jordan could see it was someone she knew.

"Dale Fadden?" Jordan said, excited and relieved.

"Jordan, we hoped we could find you! We've been traveling for days. Your message got passed along through the isolated radio operators up here. Everyone figures if they keep passing along messages, eventually someone you know may hear it. Well, I heard it and here we are. We brought several horses and we're going to ride with you the rest of the way," Fadden told her.

"Mom, who is this?" Jay asked.

"I'm sorry, this is Dale Fadden, one of the tribal leaders from the Six Nations, and I am guessing, some family members?" Jordan answered as she began to cry. "Thank you, Dale, thank you all so much."

Fadden introduced his two cousins and another council member and then they all headed back north. It took them twenty-six more days to reach Mount Katahdin in Maine where they finally emerged from the Appalachian Trail on September 12, 2012. They were now less than one hundred miles from the refuge. The journey had been rough and tiresome, with cold nights, hot and humid days, rain, fishing, hunting, and butchering their own kill. They were prepared though, and Jordan told Fadden one night around the fire,

"I never would have been prepared for this except for my job at Homeland Security, but I really didn't do anything special- our ancestors lived like this every day two hundred years ago. We are just so out of touch with the real world. We'll have to embrace it now."

"We will have to embrace that new world together, Jordan," Fadden said. "The last I heard, the U.S. had lost nearly two hundred and fifty million people from all this. We have also lost too many, and so has Canada in her bigger cities. The council has agreed that we should approach whatever is left of the chain of command of the United States and propose an alliance of our own for a new tomorrow. A new nation of nations that includes what is left of the United States, all Native American nations from Florida to the Arctic Circle, and Canada. Combined, we can be the force of freedom and democracy that the world needs now more than ever."

"I think you may be on to something, Fadden. When we get to the house, we can use the ham radio to search for Godson, Thakur and Barrett. If they're still out there, they will know what is going on."

***

Ed and the family were sitting in the outdoor kitchen listening to the emergency broadcasts when Jordan and the boys rode in on the horses, accompanied by Fadden and the others. Megan and Janice were the first to see them and ran as fast as they could across the grassy field to them, followed by everyone else at the house. Tears of joy and wild hugs abounded as Jordan looked at each one of them with her heart full of gratitude. Thomas was so overcome he fell to his knees. Tears of relief soon turned to despair when they told Jordan and the boys that they had not yet heard from Leonard or Marshal.

Fadden and the other men decided to take Jordan's offer to stay and rest for an extended time before heading back to New York. For the next several weeks, they listened to the broadcasts of troops from overseas coming home and joining the Coast Guard in hunting down remaining terrorists and restoring order. It was reported that the Coast Guard discovered yet another nuclear device in a Philadelphia apartment where an entire terrorist cell had died of the virus. The virus had spread worldwide, not only due to members of the alliance that mishandled it, but from travelers who had gotten out of the cities before the commercial flights were grounded. In many countries where health and living conditions were poor, the death toll was staggering. Even the parties with the lead roles in this unholy alliance, namely China and al Qaeda, devastated their own populations, as did most of the smaller factions. International trade ceased. Most countries were now isolated, and what was left of the United States was on its own.

Fadden located Godson and Thakur who were in charge of the entire Atlantic Command, which now consisted of all branches of U.S. troops. Godson was glad to hear that Jordan had made it through and told Fadden he would send for him when they completed the stabilization operations which Barrett was apart of. Jordan asked Godson if he had any news about Leonard or Marshal, but he didn't.

On October 31st, the family and their guests were working in the garden harvesting pumpkins, when they heard a familiar, but currently rare sound, a helicopter. Everyone walked toward the front grassy field and saw a Coast Guard helicopter hovering above. Slowly it descended until it came to rest on the ground and powered down. The door opened and out hopped Godson with a weary smile on his face followed by two more men. When the men cleared the front of the HELO, Jordan started to run; it was Leonard and Marshal. She reached them and jumped into Leonard's arms at the same time grabbing Marshal's collar. The entire family ran towards them with welcoming tears.

***

The world was forever changed. Fadden went back with Godson to the administration's new Capitol in Burlington, Vermont. Congress and most of the administration had been in D.C. during the attacks. In the line of succession to the Presidency, only the Secretary of Agriculture and the Secretary of Energy were alive. The House of Representatives, which should have four hundred thirty-five members, only had twenty-seven, and the Senate was down to nineteen from its usual one hundred. Fadden was elected to represent all the Native American Nations in North America. Canada declared full independence from Great Britain. These nations wrote a new constitution, one that still provided freedom and a participatory democracy for its people, but combined the political structure of the many free nations that were represented there. Their vision was to live freely of all entanglements to any outside entity. Leadership was voted on by this gathering of nations. There were many positions that needed to be filled, yet most governing was now going to be handled locally within towns and territories that were establishing themselves. With the meager population, anyone who had worked within the federal government would now be shuffled into the many vacant authoritative positions. Free and open elections would take place the following term. Since Godson and Thakur were now at the head of the Joint Services, Leonard was field promoted to Atlantic Commander.

Jordan decided to accept an appointment as the Cultural Liaison to the new government of The United Nations of North America.

Leonard and Jordan started their new life in Maine. Chloe and Foster were picked up by the military and brought to Marshal's current duty station in the new Capitol. Parts of North America resembled the old west. Horses, bikes, ferries and some trains provided transportation, and the military sometimes flew overhead with their jets. Local farming, local craftsmen, local manufacturing, local infrastructure and local social interactions were the order of the day. Reconstruction was going to take many years, but the spirit of freedom was vibrant and very much alive. The first night home after the gathering of the nations, Leonard and Jordan snuggled in bed.

"I kept hope that you would return, but sometimes I wondered if I was just hopelessly in denial. I love you. I don't know what I would do without you. This country has lost so much... so very much. Families, teachers, artists, scientists and the common connection we had of being Americans. We have to adapt to a new way, but at least those of us that remain are doing it together, which still makes it our way," Jordan reflected.

"I love you too. What I can't figure out is, how such a short one, who didn't eat her green beans or drink her milk when she was growing up, could have made it all that way." Leonard said softly.

Jordan smiled, walked over to the window, looked out, and watched as everyone's lights turned off for the night.

As Leonard approached her and wrapped his arms around her, she said, "I fully understand what I have, and I am forever grateful."

About the Author

Preisler Harrington is an Anthropologist who has studied current and ancient cultures and holds degrees in Anthropology and U.S. National Security.

Coming Soon

'Analyzing 2012' A.K.A. 'Analyzing Doomsday'
Be sure to look for this Companion book to *'2012 Armageddon: Unholy Alliance'* A.K.A. *'The Nuclear Sword Of Damocles'* coming in mid 2012. A non-fiction book that analyzes the Maya and other ancient civilizations, the Bible and directed prophecies, scorched earth scenarios, the counter intelligent predictions and cashing in, the real apocalypses and a reason for hope.

Made in United States
North Haven, CT
11 December 2022

28472752R00090